Evie Brooks is

Marooned

in Manhattan

SHEILA AGNEW was born in New York and grew up in Dublin with her sister and two brothers. They liked to pretend to be the children in *The Lion, The Witch and The Wardrobe*.

Although Sheila couldn't quite make it to Narnia, she set out to experience what she could of this world. After graduating from UCD., she practiced as a lawyer in London, Sydney and New York and got to work in such far-flung places as Accra, Cairo and Bratislava.

Sheila has wanted to be a writer since she was seven and fell in love with *Danny, the Champion of the World*. In 2002, she took time-out from her legal career to write and to travel around Asia. In 2011, she moved to Argentina to learn Spanish and work on a horse farm. The following year, she relocated to Dingle in County Kerry where she wrote *Evie Brooks*. Sheila based the character of 'Ben' on her own black-and-white spaniel of dubious lineage.

Sheila now lives and writes in New York City.

Evie Brooks is Marooned in Manhattan

Sheila Agnew

THE O'BRIEN PRESS
DUBLIN

First published 2014 by
The O'Brien Press Ltd,
12 Terenure Road East,
Rathgar, Dublin 6,
Ireland.
Tel: +353 1 4923333
Fax: +353 1 4922777
E-mail: books@obrien.ie
Website: www.obrien.ie

ISBN: 978-1-84717-558-8

8 7 6 5 4 3 2 1
18 17 16 15 14

Illustrations courtesy of iStockphoto
Printed and bound by CPI Group (UK) Ltd, Croydon, CR0 4YY
The paper in this book is produced using pulp from managed forests

The O'Brien Press receives assistance from

DEDICATION

For my best friend, my twin sister, Claire Gollwitzer

ACKNOWLEDGEMENTS

It takes a village to raise a children's book. My warmest gratitude to my village – my family and friends and also to Michael O'Brien, Mary Webb and the team at The O'Brien Press, Frank Fahy and the members of the 2012 Sixth Class at Scoil Mhuire, Mount Sackville, Chapelizod, Dublin 20.

Prologue

Lashing out furiously like a cornered dog, I managed to free the collar of my cardigan from the security guard's grip and started to freefall into a void, my long hair trailing swiftly behind me. It was blacker in the rubbish chute than the darkest, loneliest part of the night. The noise echoing around me was the most horrible part; the high-pitched scream of a terrified child in a blind panic. It was only later I realised I was the child and the scream came from me.

OH MY GOD! A thick clump of my hair got stuck on something protruding from one of the narrow walls of the enclosed chute.

'HELP!' I yelled, with all that I had in me. 'HELLLLLLLLLP… PLEEAASSSSE … HELP!'

But there was no response. The security guard didn't hear me or he didn't care.

I desperately reached upwards and clawed with my hands and I wriggled and kicked out frantically with my legs to try and disentangle myself, but it was no good. I was stuck alone in the dark with excruciating pain shooting through my head as the entire weight of my body rested on that band of thick hair. I couldn't move up and I couldn't move down. I was trapped in that narrow, suffocating space.

I'm going to die, I thought. Hanged by my hair until I am dead.

Just when it didn't seem possible to feel more frightened, I thought about what might be waiting for me below at the bottom of the chute. Maybe this narrow tunnel led directly to an incinerator and I would be burnt to a crisp, my skin blistering and melting in the flames until all that remained of me was a little pile of grey ashes and a mound of burnt hair.

Paralysed with fear, my efforts to release myself slowed and then stopped. All was still and very quiet. I would die soon. I knew it.

My fear ebbed and a huge sadness welled up inside me. I saw myself at the start of the summer, arriving at the airport in New York. I saw again the customs officer, a tall, handsome black man in a white shirt looking at me, a skinny, twelve-year-old Irish girl, carrying an enormous, soft, toy elephant. I took both of my passports out of my bag, the old Irish one and the new, shiny, blue American one and it was the new one I handed to him. He glanced at it and then back down at me.

'Welcome home,' he said, stamping my passport with a heavy thud.

'But I've never been to America before,' I said.

'Well, you're here now, sweetheart,' he replied with a smile.

And I saw myself on my first ride on the subway, when the

air-conditioning broke down and people sweated around me, black and white and Chinese and Native American and Hispanic, and a mother with a baby who looked like an Eskimo. Almost everyone jammed into that train complained bitterly about the humidity and poked one another with their bags and their elbows as they tried to fan themselves.

And I remembered the noise of their different languages mingling together and the long curly side ringlets and grey beard of a silent and patient old man wearing a black hat and a long black coat, and I remembered the sour smell of sweat. I was thinking that if an alien landed in New York, it would be impossible to convince him that we were all the same species, all human.

I felt very, very tired. I closed my eyes.

'You're going to be ok, Evie,' whispered my mum's voice in the void.

'Mum?' I said, my eyes snapping open and straining in the darkness to see, but there was nothing, which was okay, because much as I missed Mum, I'm sure I would die instantly of a heart attack if I saw her ghost.

'Think, Evie, think,' Mum's voice urged. 'What did Uncle Scott do to your hair?'

I gasped. Digging around in my left pocket, I pulled out the small nail scissors I had used that morning to trim Ben's nails and, reaching my left arm upwards, tugged the scissors frantically through my hair.

Snip. Snip. Snip. Snip.

Freefalling again through space, feeling light as an Aero.

'Owwwwwwwww!' I exclaimed, as I landed with a heavy bump in a large metal rubbish skip filled with black plastic garbage bags.

I gazed upwards for a moment.

'Thank you, Mum!' I mouthed silently.

Chapter 1

I am an orphan. That should mean I have magical powers or a fabulously wealthy grandfather who owns a travelling three-ring circus or a five-star hotel in Morocco. At the very least, I should have a destined-to-be-a-star singing voice. Fat chance. In fact, my singing is so hideous that one of my teachers instructed me to whisper the words during choir practice because I was throwing the other kids off-key.

It was Mrs Scanlon's idea that I keep a journal, but I only write in it when I feel like it. She is the child psychologist I had to visit every week when Mum got sick. Mum meant well but when you are made to see a therapist, it is blindingly obvious that things are about to get so much worse. Mrs Scanlon had very long, scraggly grey hair, a face like a badger – a *kind* badger; and an interesting preference for multicoloured gypsy skirts. Practically the very first thing she asked me was, 'How do you feel about your mum being sick?'

'Bad!' I said, my mouth falling slightly open in amazement. To think that poor Mum forked out loads of cash we could not afford just so I could spend forty-five minutes every week humouring Mrs Scanlon and assembling puzzles intended for kids half my age. Mum died seven weeks and two days after the first session so I did not have to go see Mrs Scanlon anymore. I almost miss her.

Soon after Mum went into the hospital for the last time, she told me I would be leaving Ireland to live with her brother, my Uncle Scott, in New York. That floored me and I thought, no way, but what kind of person would fight with their dying mother? Except maybe for Amy McCann, who is in my class at school. I kept my mouth firmly shut, which was not an easy thing to do.

I didn't know Scott but that was not his fault. Every time we planned to visit him in New York, something would happen, like Mum would unexpectedly get a new part in a play. That's not completely accurate. Scott sent us the money for the plane fares twice, but we could not resist spending it on other things, like a drum kit for me and highlights and burgundy cowboy boots for Mum.

Scott came to Dublin to say goodbye to Mum and he stayed for the funeral. He has the exact same colouring as Mum: dirty blonde hair minus Mum's highlights, and eyes so intensely blue that everyone stares at him for a few extra seconds when they first meet him. He is much taller than she was and has the kind of skin that suggests he just got back from a holiday in the Canaries. Mum often said that Scott was born cool, but until I met him, I figured she just said that because he's her older brother. He's not a loud American at all. He must have noticed that I avoided him as much as possible but he didn't ask me any silly questions or try to pretend everything was normal and okay, and he said calling him just 'Scott' without the 'Uncle' was fine.

I will skip over the funeral part because I can't bear to write about it just now – maybe later, maybe never. The morning after the funeral, Scott and I wandered around the flat on North Great George's Street in Dublin, bumping into each other and saying 'sorry'. It didn't feel like home any-more with Mum gone. I tried to figure out how to tell Scott that I had no intention of heading off to America with him. I wanted to stay in Ireland where I belonged. I wanted to live with my godmother, Mum's best friend, Janet. But no clever ideas came into my head; they never do when you need them and so, finally, I just blurted out, 'I'm sorry. I don't want to sound mean or ungrateful but I'm not going with you to New York. I am staying here with Janet. That's kind of the whole point of having a godparent, that's the person who brings you up, you know, if something happens and your parents are not on the scene.'

Scott sat down beside me on our ugly brown sofa that sags in the middle, but not too close, and ran his hand through his hair quickly so that it stood up in spikes.

'Evie, I'm not a military dictator from some banana repub-lic. I'd never force you into going anywhere you didn't want to go. But I think you would like New York if you gave it a chance. Alicia wanted you to live with me. She says so in her will. She made me your guardian. A guardian is basically the chief godparent.'

I didn't have a clue how to respond to that. First, I'm not

sure what a banana republic is. Second, it was pretty clever of Scott to drag Mum into the conversation. It didn't feel right in my stomach to be defying her wishes but I couldn't believe that Scott really wanted me even if I wanted to go, which I most definitely did not. Scott is thirty-six but he's not married and he doesn't have any kids of his own.

'I don't want to cramp your style by going to live with you,' I said.

'I don't have a style,' Scott said, 'and you won't be cramping anything. We are family.'

I pretended to watch TV even though the volume was turned down too low to hear. Scott continued, 'You don't have to come straight away. You can stay with Janet until the end of month so you can finish out the school year and be with your friends. Then you can come visit me for the summer, just for the summer; if you don't like it, you can come back to Ireland in September.'

I felt suspicious. When an adult says something that sounds fair and reasonable, there's usually a catch of some kind.

'Scott,' I said, 'I know I'm not going to like living in New York. I'm Irish. My teacher told us that Irish children are not brought up like cows to be exported to a foreign country. I *definitely* would want to come home at the end of the summer. How do I know you will let me?'

Scott thought about this for a minute or two and then he called Janet who was pretending to be busy making toast in the kitchen, but was obviously shamelessly eavesdropping. As soon as she bustled into the living room, her silver bracelets jangling, Scott turned to me, 'Evie, I promise you, with Janet as the witness, if you want to come back to Ireland in September, you can and nobody will stop you. In fact, I will make sure that happens.'

'You will *always* be welcome to live with me,' added Janet. 'I would love to have you and I'm only prepared to let you go because that's what your mum wanted.'

'Thank you,' I said and my eyes felt itchy. I rubbed them vigorously, automatically waiting for Mum to tell me to stop rubbing my eyes, but of course she couldn't. Scott got up and walked to the fireplace, where, with his hands in his pockets and his back to me, he began to look through the many photographs of Mum and me scattered across the mantelpiece. He gave a little nod to Janet who meekly returned to the kitchen.

I didn't want to trust Scott, but I wasn't feeling overwhelmed with options. Janet wouldn't be able to keep me without Scott's consent. My savings amounted to fifty-seven Euro and some change. I didn't have a credit card or any living relatives that I knew of other than Scott. I wouldn't even be thirteen for another nine months (my birthday is 7 February). The police don't allow twelve-year-olds to live by themselves and, even if they did, I would be way too scared to live alone.

'Ok,' I said in a little voice and Scott whipped around to face me.

'Just until September,' I added, a little louder, and held out my hand to Scott to shake on it, but he awkwardly high-fived it instead.

Janet appeared immediately in the doorway and giggled a bit for no reason, a dead giveaway that she fancies Scott. Janet is not very good with men. Nor was Mum. That was a big bond between them. I have a feeling I will not be good with them either.

Take John Donaghy from school, for example, super cute, with light brown hair and shiny brown eyes. He talks very quickly with his hands when he is excited and he can sketch anyone in the world in a few minutes with a pencil stub.

I spent all last summer learning to climb the big tree in the park behind the junior infants' school. Every evening between five and half past six, John used to cycle by and there I'd be, sitting on the bottom branch, coolly reading a book. If no other boys were with him, he'd wave to me, but that was it. Once, I even manoeuvred myself so that, as he passed by, I hung upside down with my legs curled over the branch, but he just waved as usual and I very nearly fell when I waved back. After all of that hard work to impress him, when we went back to school in September, he started going with Hannah Cunningham, who would never in a trillion years be able to climb that tree.

Hannah is very pretty, like a Spanish exchange student. I am in the middle of my class when it comes to height, but I am mainly made up of legs, which not even Mum could say is cute. They are far too skinny and bony; at our class outing to Glendalough last year, Amy McCann called me Daddy Longlegs in front of the whole bus and then she had the cheek to repeat it on Facebook, but it didn't catch on, thank God.

Hannah Cunningham's hair is caramel coloured and curly and short. Mine reaches half way down my back; it is boot polish black and when it's not riddled with pesky knots that appear overnight, it is straight without even a hint of a curl. To top it off, I have freckles. Hannah doesn't have one freckle, not even on her arms or anything. I suppose it would be fair to say that I have interesting eyes. They are large and grey and they can look lighter or darker, depending on my mood.

Last year, Mum played the part of the youngest sister in a play by Chekhov (that's an old, dead Russian guy), called *Three Sisters*. One night backstage, I overheard the middle one of the *Three Sisters* say, 'Alicia's daughter, Evie, has a real promise of beauty.'

But the older Sister, who was a pathetic actress and only got the part because she was the girlfriend of the director's brother, replied, 'She could go either way, ugly or beautiful.'

I didn't find that comforting.

I noticed Scott examining a photograph of Mum and me dressed up for Halloween last year. I was *Alice in Wonderland* and Mum wore ripped fishnet tights and a little miniskirt as the Queen of Tarts instead of the Queen of Hearts. Not everyone got her costume, but I thought it was brilliant.

Scott looked sad. It is always so much scarier when adults are sad.

'Do you have a girlfriend, Scott?' I asked to try and get him to think about someone other than Mum.

'Sort of,' he said. 'We've been dating a few months, so yeah, I guess Leela is my girlfriend. You'll meet her.'

'You'll like her,' he added a few seconds later, a little unconvincingly.

I didn't find that very comforting either.

Chapter 2

I missed a few weeks of writing in my journal. I was a bit overwhelmed by America. Scott lives on West 77th Street on the Upper West Side of Manhattan, between Columbus Avenue and Central Park West. Manhattan has two names; it's called Manhattan or New York City. That's confusing and it took me a while to figure it out. Manhattan is an island but it doesn't feel like an island at all. It's important to know on the subway whether you want to go uptown or downtown. Otherwise, you will probably waste a lot of time riding in the wrong direction. That has happened to me several times already, but I'm getting the hang of it now.

Scott's street is very clean and wide and lined with trees. His side of the street is full of high, posh, apartment buildings with marble lobbies, but you hardly ever see anyone going in or out. The whole block on the other side of the street is taken up with the Museum of Natural History, which has life-sized dinosaur skeletons and lots of other cool stuff, like a butterfly conservatory. I imagined a room full of musty glass cases displaying sad, stiff, dead butterflies. I couldn't have been more wrong. The butterfly exhibition has hundreds, maybe even a thousand live butterflies flying around. Some of them have wings in colours that I didn't know even existed, like vermilion and cattleya.

Central Park, which everyone just calls *the Park,* is right at the end of the block. If you walk in the Park entrance at West 77th Street and turn left and walk down a steep hill, you'll find a fair-sized stream with a wooden plank footbridge. Beyond the bridge is a gigantic, bulky, leafy tree, which has a very wide, low branch that runs along a few centimetres off the ground. It's a perfect place to hang out. To the left winds a dirt and pebble path lined with old-fashioned lampposts that leads under a stone bridge. When the lights come on as dusk falls, you can very easily fool yourself into believing that you are in Narnia if you have even the tiniest scrap of imagination.

Six doormen work in Scott's building in shifts. Their job is to open the doors for you and give you your dry-cleaning and any FedEx packages that arrive. It's gas. Scott says that they also clear out the snow in front of the building in winter. They are very knowledgeable about almost everything and everyone. They phone you when your food is delivered.

They are super friendly. They nicknamed me 'Irish' and they call out, 'How is Irish doing today?' or 'Good morning, Beautiful!' which is a great start to any day. They often slip me candy, which is what they call sweets here. The Cadbury's chocolate bars they sell in New York taste gross, like someone thought it would be a great idea to add gravy mix to them. Frank has a very thick, brown moustache. He is always joking around so I think he is probably my favourite doorman, but they are all kind and funny, except for Romy who can have a bit of an attitude. He is from Bulgaria and sometimes he pretends he cannot speak English, although his English is almost perfect.

Scott is a vet, which I found intriguing. I have never owned a dog or a cat because we always had landlords who were not pet-friendly. Mum eventually got me a goldfish, but it only lived for a few days so she got me another one and it died after a few weeks and we flushed him down the loo as well. It was not particularly sad; Mum actually had a fit of the giggles at the second send-off, which she tried to disguise as a coughing fit. I don't know if I could really bond with a fish; a dolphin, definitely, but a fish is not overburdened with personality.

Scott's practice is called *Upper West Side Veterinary*. He totally knows that is a crap name, not original at all, and he's thinking about my suggestion of calling it *Scott's Super Vet: Treating Snakes through Stoats*. But he says that loads of New Yorkers do not know what a stoat is so he would probably get people turning up in the middle of the night looking for a doctor to treat their strep throats.

Scott says that you can tell a lot about the owners and their lives just by what kind of pet they have. For example, if they have a Great Dane or an Irish Wolfhound or some other really large dog, like a Newfoundland, then they probably live in a studio apartment the size of a very large bathroom. On the other hand, if they have a Chihuahua, which is a tiny toy dog, then they probably live in a four-storey house or a penthouse.

The practice is open from 8am to 7pm on Mondays through Fridays and from 9am to 2pm on Saturdays. Three evenings a week and every other Sunday, Scott is on-call for emergencies. On my second night here, Mrs Rubinstein called him on his cell phone to go around to her apartment because Lulu, her Siamese cat, had diarrhoea.

Scott asked, 'How long has it been going on?'

Mrs Rubenstein spoke so loudly that I heard her reply.

'It has not actually started yet, Doctor, but Lulu has that face she gets when she feels a bout of diarrhoea coming on. Could you please come straight away? I am terrified she might die of dehydration.'

Scott did an excellent imitation of Lulu's 'possibly getting diarrhoea' face at me. He told me later that Mrs Rubenstein is a terrific old lady, but she is a hypochondriac when it comes to her cat.

Scott's apartment is on the ground floor. It has a large combined living room and kitchen with a wide flat screen TV that takes up almost an entire wall. On the opposite wall is a giant photograph of an enormous concrete swimming pool without any water in it. A rock concert is taking place in the pool and you could spend hours looking at all the different, interesting-looking people attending the concert. There is an unpainted oak table with benches that look like logs, a long black leather couch and a small, high glass table with three bar stools with a framed painting of a herd of buffalo behind it.

In the middle of the living room, a spiral, twisty iron staircase leads down to his veterinary practice, which is in the basement and has a separate entrance at the front of the building – a green door at the bottom of nine steps. Beside the spiral staircase is a fireman's pole so when Scott has an animal emergency he can just slide down it. He told me he was going to get rid of it because it was too dangerous, but I begged him not to because it is my favourite thing in the apartment. He told me not to mention the stairs or the fireman's pole to anyone because he never got around to getting the permits for building them.

There is a narrow hallway leading from the living room to a big bedroom (Scott's room), and then there's a closet-sized middle room (where freakily tidy Scott keeps his clothes, including eight pairs of jeans), a bathroom and, finally, my bedroom, which is pretty small but has a cool slanted roof and a triangular window. The walls are painted light pink and the bedspread is hot pink and there's a little white desk with a pink and white striped chair and a large cushion/bean bag squashy thing in turquoise with pink roses. I had to bite my lip because I'm not a huge fan of pink of any shade, but it was really nice of Scott to make the effort and so I just said thank you. Now, I wonder if I'm going to be stuck for the whole summer pretending that I like pink.

When I went to bed the first night, Scott stuck his head into my room and said, 'I think Ben wants to sleep with you, if that's ok?' and I said, 'Sure'.

Ben is Scott's dog and I thought it would be like sleeping with a soft toy, but having a warm, living, breathing dog sleeping with his head on your feet is nothing like going to bed with a stuffed teddy. Ben is a five-year old Sprocker, which is a cross-breed, half English springer spaniel and half cocker spaniel. He is black with a white muzzle with black freckles on it and a very wet, black nose. He has incredibly long, droopy, black ears. They seem to be of very little use as he hardly ever comes when he is called, unless food is involved. He has the softest fur that you can imagine. He weighs about the same as a Monday morning schoolbag so he's a bit heavy. His favourite toy is a faded bluish/yellowish, fluffy and none-too-clean duck/pheasant/bird thing named Martha. Ben carries Martha around in his mouth a lot, chewing on her in an absentminded way. When he's not chewing on her, he likes to keep her in his food bowl, although sometimes he forgets and she turns up in the oddest places.

Scott works with another vet called Doctor Barrett, but she told me straight off to call her Joanna. She has long, silky, dark red hair and gorgeous hazel eyes, framed by black rectangular glasses. All of her clothes are black, except once I saw her in a greyish sweater. It is possible that the sweater was black once and had just faded in the wash.

Joanna has read all the *Harry Potter* books and Ron Weasley is her favourite character. Her boyfriend's name is Stefan and he's from Frankfurt in Germany, but has lived in New York for five years.

On my third night in America, after Joanna had sushi with

me and Scott and they were both impressed by my use of chopsticks (as if we don't have sushi in Dublin), she tripped on Martha and fell halfway down the spiral staircase with a sickening thud-thudding sound, but no screaming. I really admired Joanna a lot because she picked herself up straight away, with no whining at all, just looking very flustered and pink in the face and said, 'It's an unusually light evening on the wine front when I do *not* fall down the stairs.'

And she said with just a hint of sarcasm that she hoped she had not hurt Martha by stepping on her.

Scott was doing that useless guy thing where he kept asking Joanna if she was ok and did she think she should go to the hospital just in case she had broken any bones when it was obvious that she just wanted to forget about the fall because it was so embarrassing. She kept saying she was fine and he said maybe she had a sprain and we should get it checked out. Finally, she yelled, 'Just shut up about it!' but she used a curse word as well and then she used it again because she was so upset about saying it in the first place in front of me.

I said it was fine. 'Janet was always saying *effing* this or that,' which made Scott laugh and Joanna joined in. I'm glad I helped break the tension.

Not everyone is as cool as Joanna. Scott's girlfriend, Leela, is beyond painful. She is always moaning about being stressed. She's a divorce attorney – when marriages break up, she argues in court on behalf of her client about splitting up the money and the kids. The way she talks about it, you would think she is chopping up the kids like mincemeat with one of Scott's incredibly sharp Japanese butcher's knives.

Leela has long, super shiny, straight dark hair and dark eyes with incredibly long eyelashes and she is so beautiful that men in the street stare at her, and if they don't, she will pause and laugh or speak a little louder or toss her hair until they do. She is short, but looks tall, because she wears skyscraper heels.

During my first week, I got up in the middle of the night for a glass of water and I bumped into her in the hall wearing a flimsy, see-through nightgown and she still had heels on. She screamed so loudly when she saw me that I dropped the glass of water. If anyone had the right to scream, it was me.

I thought at first from the self-important way Leela acted all the time that she might genuinely have some kind of connection to Indian royalty, or to a celebrity, but Joanna snorted when I mentioned this and said that she is only a *princess* from New Jersey, whose parents emigrated from Mumbai in India when she was a baby.

The thing that probably bugs me most is that Leela just pretends to like animals when Scott is around. Whenever she drops by, which even Scott thinks is too often, she always makes a big fuss of Ben, but when Scott is on the phone, she totally ignores him. One time when Scott was in the bathroom and Ben put his paws on her knees and dumped Martha in her lap, she screamed like she'd been burned. I've never heard anyone scream as much as she does. She was pretty mean to poor Ben, who was only trying to be friendly,

26

yelling at him to get off her and giving him a little kick with one of her stilettos. Then she washed her hands in a very vigorous way as if he had fleas, sighing melodramatically the whole time. Ben's got such a good heart, though, because he always forgives her and is nice to her. I try to be nice to her because Scott asked me to, but I don't have Ben's temperament so it's not always easy, especially when she calls me 'sweetie' and it's so fake that I feel like screaming myself.

Chapter 3

The small waiting room is nearly always crowded. Some of the patients interact happily, sniffing each other's butts while their owners exchange details of their pets' histories. Others are cautious or aloof. Pet owners in New York City usually refer to themselves as '*Mommies*' or '*Daddies*'. But I can't imagine Mr Fannelli ever referring to himself as his dog's *Daddy*. He has a chocolate-brown Labrador called Spike, who frequently suffers from stomach-aches on account of eating loads of crap that he should not be eating. One Monday morning, he chomped down an entire, colossal bag of marshmallows intended for Mr Fannelli's grandchildren.

'Mr Fannelli,' said Scott. 'Meet my new assistant, my niece, Miss Evangeline Brooks.'

I was wearing the official-looking white coat Joanna had given me, with the sleeves rolled up.

'Hi, Mr Fannelli!' I piped up.

'Ah, from the old country, from Scotland, are you?' he asked.

'No, Dublin, Ireland,' I pointed out.

'It is a beautiful town, Cork.'

'Well, Cork is not really near Dublin ...', but I had lost Mr Fannelli's attention, which was focused on the scales. Scott grunted a little as he lifted Spike onto them. Mr Fannelli looked distinctly guilty. Scott laid a hand on his shoulder.

'One hundred and forty-two pounds, Mr Fannelli. Spike has been overindulging again. Has he vomited up the marsh-mallows yet?'

'No, but I gave him a couple of spoons of Pepto-Bismol.' Scott sighed.

'Mr Fannelli, we have talked about this before, many, many times. You should not give Pepto-Bismol to dogs on a regular basis. Let's get Spike up on the examining table.'

But Mr Fannelli held back.

'I think I will take a seat in the waiting room. The rheumatism in my left knee is acting up again,' and he shuffled off.

I followed Scott into the examining room and together we managed to haul Spike up onto the table. Joanna was sitting on a stool by the window, peering at some slides under a microscope. She glanced in our direction.

'Ah, Spike again, looking a bit sorry for himself.'

'Wow, that's a very cool dress,' I said.

She smiled at me, jumped up from the stool and did a sexy twirl, her right hand holding her glasses in place.

'Stefan is taking me to *Azure Sea* tonight.'

'What's that?' I wondered.

'A ridiculously overpriced, purportedly romantic restaurant created by the same guy who did the Hallmark app,' Scott interjected.

Joanna ignored him. Scott gently palpated Spike's tummy. Just as Joanna came over to give us a hand, Spike opened his mouth and projectile vomited a long stream of gooey, grey-ish whitish stuff that just missed Joanna's silky black slip dress, with one big gob splattering on my Converse runners. Scott did not even get a dribble.

Joanna squealed.

'Pity he missed,' Scott said cheerfully. 'That should have nicely masked the overpowering aroma of flowers and sea-weed in *Azure Sea*.'

Joanna shot him one of her best dirty looks. Spike belched loudly. He seemed much better.

'This dress cost three hundred and seven-five dollars,' Joanna pointed out. 'And I don't suppose Mr Fannelli would have paid for the dry cleaning'.

'Mr Fannelli, who hasn't paid a bill since the ark reached dry land?' Scott replied. 'Which reminds me, we have to talk to him about that.'

Joanna shot him another dirty look.

'*We* do not have to do anything. *You* do it. And Spike is your patient. Last week, I had to ring Mrs Sobelsohn about her overdue bills, and she kept me on the phone for half an hour. I ultimately ended up agreeing to spay her new cat for free.' And she walked out.

Scott watched her go.

'Joanna is Canadian,' he said meaningfully, but I have no idea what that is supposed to mean. Scott always says that when he doesn't know what to say about Joanna. I gave

Spike a pat just as Ben trotted in, his nose sensing that he might be missing an adventure of some kind. And, this is very gross, but we had to clean up the remnants of Spike's sick very quickly because otherwise Ben would probably try and gobble it up. Since I have witnessed Ben trying to eat his own puke, I can't imagine he would be overly fussy about eating another dog's.

Yesterday, I got a new pet, a brown-green turtle named Sam. He just looked like a *Sam*. He is a common snapping turtle who used to live near Turtle Pond in Central Park. I was walking through the Ramble, which is a wild part of the Park little visited by tourists. Rounding a corner with high mulberry bushes, I was shocked when I saw three kids in skateboarding clothes torturing a poor turtle by stretching it between them. One boy and the girl had his front legs and the other boy with greasy blonde hair held both of the back legs. I ran right up to them and tried to grab the turtle out of their hands.

'What are you creeps doing to that turtle? STOP it right now.'

But they just sniggered at me. The greaseball boy pushed me on my shoulder so hard that I nearly fell over. So I pinched him as hard as I could on his arm and he yelled and grabbed me and forced my hands behind my back. I was too furious to be scared.

'Let me go, let me go right now or I'm going to call the police.'

The smaller boy with the red t-shirt laughed.

'Let me go, let me go,' he chanted, mocking my accent.

'Shut up, Carlos' said the girl, who was stocky and had red sunglasses, and for an instant I thought I had an ally.

'We were wondering' she said slowly, 'how long it would take for the snapping turtle to snap, but now that you are here, let's try stretching you instead.'

She and Carlos tried to pick up my legs as the greaseball kept a tight hold on my arms. I kicked out as hard as I could, managing to connect with Carlos's face. He swore and wiped his bleeding lip. As I continued to struggle, they hoisted me up in the air and the indignity was worse than the pain.

Then the greaseball yelled in pain and shock as a tall boy, wearing a Rangers cap, grabbed him from behind, pulled him off me and knocked him to the ground. He staggered quickly to his feet and then the horrible coward ran off, without even waiting to see what happened to his friends, who had dropped my legs, so that I crashed to the ground with such force that I struggled to breathe.

'Get out of here, freaks!' the Rangers boy commanded in a quiet but scary voice and they left, the girl turning around and flipping her finger at us.

'Are you ok?' the Rangers boy asked me.

I nodded and started to struggle to my feet.

'Whoa,' he said, and bent down, locked his arms around me and pulled me gently to my feet. 'Anything broken?'

I shook my head again.

'Do you speak?' he asked.

I nodded and he grinned, a lopsided grin.

'I'm fine,' I said, gasping a little, 'the turtle.'

The Rangers boy bent down to examine the tortured turtle that had tried to crawl away from the scene but didn't get far with one very limp back leg.

'I think this little guy needs a vet. There's a good one right near here, Dr Brooks. He'll help.'

I felt so proud.

'He's my uncle. He's cool, he has a Harley but he can't ride it just now because it needs work.'

'Ok,' the boy muttered and he pulled his ringing cell phone out of his pocket.

'What's up?' and he waved distractedly at me.

'Bye kid, go back to your mommy and get her to take you and your turtle to your uncle. You shouldn't be wandering around in the Ramble by yourself,' and he casually walked away, still talking on his cell phone.

I didn't even get the chance to say thank you or find out his name.

'Bye *kid*', like I was six years old or something. Who did he think he was, striding around the Park like he was Spiderman or something, rescuing people who didn't need his help and then calling them '*kid*' and telling them to go back to their mommies?

I should have said, 'Oh sure, oops! I can't because she's DEAD.'

To be fair, I hadn't had the situation totally under control. '*He's cool, he has a Harley.*'

I bit my bottom lip as I remembered my blabbing. The

Rangers guy must think I am a total weirdo, a baby and a weirdo. I picked up the turtle gently. The fight seemed to have gone out of him because he didn't try to bite me, or maybe he sensed I was trying to help him. I wrapped him in the bottom of my t-shirt and headed home.

Scott did an x-ray, which confirmed that Sam had a broken leg. He sedated him and pulled the leg back in place and bandaged it.

'Right, there's not much more we can do. It's not like when a human breaks a leg, we can't put a cast on it. We can just make him comfortable and, in six to eight weeks, he can go back to his merry life in Turtle Pond.'

'Thank you,' I said.

I had told Scott that I just happened to come across Sam in the Park, which was trueish. I left out the part about the skateboarder bullies and the Rangers boy. Scott might try to baby me and stop me from going around by myself during the day. Besides, sometimes it's nice to have a secret that belongs to nobody but you; you can lie on your bed and take it out and think about it whenever you like.

I did ask Scott, 'Are the Rangers a basketball or a baseball team?'

'Sacrilege!' he exclaimed. 'They are the greatest professional ice hockey team in the world. They're *our* team, from New York. They play at Madison Square Garden. I'll take you to a game in the fall when the season starts.'

'Thanks very much, but I won't be here then,' I reminded him.

'Oh yeah, I forgot, too bad!' said Scott and he started to wipe down the examining table with disinfectant, whistling in an irritating manner a catchy tune I did not recognise.

Chapter 4

We ate Indian food last night, which Leela brought in little plastic containers, Bhindi Anardana and Sarson Ka Saag and Aloo Gobi and potato and chick pea samosas. Leela told us that she is putting together a cookery book with tips about getting divorced because it is a simple and surefire way to celebrity and easy money.

'What's the difference between *putting together* a book and writing one?' I asked curiously.

Leela glared at me and ignored my question.

'I am going to call it, *Healthy and Delicious Vegetarian Indian Meals for Divorced or Separated Dads*.'

'Why not mothers as well?' Joanna asked.

Leela snickered and said, 'Women don't tend to like me because they are jealous of the way I look.'

'There is something true in that,' said Joanna as she got up, stacked her plate very noisily into the dishwater and left, muttering something about having years of laundry to do. Leela watched her go, still rambling on about what she called her book concept. She thought she should wear a traditional sari, but in white with silver accents, in the photograph on the front cover of the book.

'Tasty and tasteful,' she said, glancing at Scott.

He didn't respond because he was devouring the samosas while sleeping with his eyes open, a talent that drives Joanna and Leela nuts. It's probably the only thing they have in common, apart from being women.

Leela is Hindu. She said she doesn't eat meat because it is against her religion.

I said, 'In Ireland, years and years ago, people didn't eat meat on Fridays because Jesus died on Good Friday. Janet's father, my honorary grandfather, still doesn't eat meat on Fridays but he has a huge fry-up with tons of bacon and sausages on Saturday mornings.'

Leela didn't look very interested in Janet's dad's eating habits but she said, 'Cows are very sacred animals in India.'

Scott woke up and said that sometimes he wished he had a country practice so he could treat cows and horses and other farmyard animals.

The phone rang and I raced to get it.

'This is Jeremy Humphrey, I need the vet to come right now because my goat is acting weird,' the caller announced.

'Your, em, goat?' I asked.

'Yes, G-O-A-T, my goat.'

I think Scott gets to treat more farmyard animals than he realises. I've been trying hard to be a helpful assistant and already I know I need to get details of the symptoms to help Scott with the diagnosis.

'What do you mean exactly by "acting weird"?' I asked politely.

37

Mr Humphrey sounded annoyed.

'Weird weird. Tell Dr Brooks to come straight away. He knows where I live, and don't send the chick, I want the man vet!' and he hung up. It was a good thing that Joanna didn't hear him because she wouldn't have been impressed.

Scott was already heading downstairs to get his bag of instruments and medicines. It's not a black bag like the medical bags used by doctors in movies. It's a bright blue sports bag. I rushed to catch up with him while Leela whined about being left alone with nothing to do. We walked quickly, the way everyone walks in Manhattan, towards Mr Humphrey's place on West End Avenue and 74th Street but slowed down on the last block because Scott said he felt bloated.

Mr Humphrey lives alone in the ground floor apartment with a large back garden. He buzzed us in and we walked through the apartment to the back yard. Mr Humphrey's goat is a dark caramel colour, and, his name is Billy, which, I mentioned to Scott, is pretty much up there with calling a collie Lassie.

'Or a Great Dane, Scooby Doo,' he answered.

'I had no *idea* Scooby Doo was a Great Dane.'

The only goats I had ever seen before were at petting zoos. Billy took me by surprise because he was so small. Scott explained that he is a 'pygmy goat', a type of goat which first came to the United States from West Africa in the 1950s. He said that Mr Humphrey had trained Billy really well to walk on a leash and he is very docile and friendly.

Poor Billy was lying on the straw in a little shed and he

panted as if he had run a marathon. Mr Humphrey whistled softly in an anxious way and stroked Billy gently on his stomach. I helped hold Billy's head while Scott opened his mouth and showed us how pale the gums were. 'I think Billy has a parasite in his stomach called barber's pole worm.'

Parasites. Uuugh! Even the word made me feel like vomiting but I held it in check because I didn't want Scott to think I was too wimpy for this kind of work. We collected some of Billy's goat pellets in a little tube to send off to the laboratory to make sure Scott's diagnosis was correct. Picking up goat pooh is not the most glamorous side of the job.

'Mr Humphrey, I am going to give Billy a drench but we seem to have caught the condition fairly early and Billy should be able to make a full recovery,' Scott said, matter-of-factly.

A smile spread across Mr Humphrey's face; he's the first American I have met with yellow teeth. I thought about collecting some extra goat pellets. I was sure they could be potentially useful at some point in dealing with Leela, but Mr Humphrey had a suspicious eye on me so I restrained myself.

Later that night, I tidied my room because the next day was Thursday, which is the day Eurdes, Scott's cleaner, comes. She's not a big fan of Ben's, because of his tendency to drink noisily from the toilet bowl when he is too lazy to go to his own water bowl and also because his hair can be found in the strangest places. Ben has two main enemies, the sinister-looking striped black and orange cat called 'Mindy' from

Apartment 4L and Eurdes's vacuum cleaner. Ben is terrified of them both and runs away whenever he sees them, after a few protest barks. Bravery is not his strong suit.

Eurdes always turns up on time, at 10am sharp. On very hot days, even with the AC on, she removes her blouse and works in her bra and skirt. She has the most enormous breasts I have ever seen. I like Eurdes's bras. They are very shiny and colourful, usually bright purple or neon pink with black lace. Scott enjoys looking at them too but he has to pretend he doesn't notice. He's not very good at that.

Scott is obsessively tidy, so Eurdes's job became much harder since my arrival. Scott was pretty disgusted when he discovered that I didn't make my bed. One morning, he told me, 'It's not fair of you to expect Eurdes to do it for you.'

That surprised me and hurt my feelings because I didn't remotely expect Eurdes to make my bed. I didn't expect anyone to do it. But I started making my own bed and I have to admit Scott was right because, strangely, it's a lot nicer to get into a bed that is already made.

Chapter 5

Joanna's best friend is Rachel. She's from Boston but went to a famous college for women in New York, called Sarah Lawrence. I think they let men go there now. Rachel is the manager and part owner of a tiny art gallery on the Upper East Side. Joanna took me there to visit and Rachel gave us a tour of the paintings, which she called artworks. They were not interesting at all. I like pictures with people or animals or stormy seas with little boats or colourful strange shapes and splotches. The pictures in the gallery were of very tame fields and valleys, painted in neutral colours of muted browns and olive greens. I had to turn my head away so Rachel wouldn't see me suppressing a yawn.

After the tour, Rachel brought us to her little office upstairs for some drinks. She and Joanna drank a bottle of Prosecco between them and I had real iced tea with mint and lemon. Rachel is single and has a daughter, Kylie, who is four months older than me. Kylie arrived while I was still drinking my first iced tea and she swept me away with her downstairs to the basement. This was being used as a storage area for dozens of canvases in all shapes and sizes, which were stacked up against the walls. We sat on some packing crates. I felt a little shy so Kylie did most of the talking.

She was adopted from the province of Guangdong in China when she was two and a half years old, but she can't remember living in China or meeting her mom, Rachel, for the first time or the flight to America. Nor can she speak a word of Mandarin, but she intends to learn. She is extraordinarily pretty, with delicate features and black hair with a streak of pink on the left side near the front, and black eyes with thin, arched eyebrows. She has a short, choppy fringe, which she called *bangs*. When she smiles, she looks like someone has just told her an amazing secret. She is slender and graceful and even though she is much taller than me, her feet are about two sizes smaller. She has the most beautiful, gurgling, musical laugh I have ever heard.

She nearly had a brother last year. She doesn't know his real name so she and her mom called him Luca. He was being adopted from India and he was supposed to be six or seven years old. She and her mom had plane tickets to go to India to collect him, but a couple of weeks before the trip, the Indian authorities told them that medical tests on his wrists showed that Luca was in fact thirteen years old but so malnourished that he looked much younger. The Indian government doesn't allow children over twelve to be adopted.

'That's terrible,' I said. 'Poor Luca.'

'I know,' Kylie replied solemnly. 'When I'm eighteen I'm going to travel to India and try to find him.'

'You can come with me if you want,' she added and she also invited me to her apartment the next day.

Scott and Leela dropped me off the following morning on their way to New Jersey for a birthday lunch for Leela's mother. I was very impressed with Kylie's bedroom. She owns more clothes than all of the girls in my old class in Dublin put together. Her bedroom is painted purple and orange, and almost everything in it is purple and orange because those are her favourite colours, but if she were forced to choose between them to save her life, she would choose purple. Nina, the babysitter, gave us little plastic pots of baby carrots with hummus and glasses of cranberry-grape juice. We spent most of the morning playing dancing on Wii. Kylie is a much better dancer than I am and I'm not being modest. The streak in her hair was green this morning, not pink, and she showed me her hair highlighters in seven colours, which wash out very easily. She said that a royal blue streak would look cute on me so I let her highlight a big chunk of my hair that fell down over the right side of my face.

Kylie appraised her work and said in a satisfied voice, 'It's a statement.'

After a couple of hours, Nina walked with us over to the West Side and we stopped in a crowded bakery for cupcakes. After much agonising, Kylie chose a red velvet one but I had the banana pudding because it tastes like happiness, far better than all the cupcakes. Kylie talked about school as we ate.

'I'm so bad at math, which really sucks because, since I'm Asian, everyone thinks I should be good at math but I'm not.'

'I'm crap at maths,' I admitted.

'What are mats?' asked Kylie in a puzzled voice. 'Do you mean mat weaving classes, because my mom went to those? She bought a loom but she got fed up so now we just store her loom in the basement because she thinks she will start weaving again when she has more time.'

Kylie rolled her eyes at me.

'No, no,' I said, laughing. 'I meant mathematics. What subjects do you like?'

'I like ice-skating and dance classes but we don't do them at school; I have private classes,' Kylie said. 'I'm going to be famous and have the frozen chocolate milkshake at Serendipity every day and go to all the movie premières and the best parties and I'll wear custom ice-skating costumes designed by the coolest designers.'

'What about the people who will follow you all the time and try to photograph you when you have toilet paper stuck to your shoe?' I asked.

'The paparazzi?' she said, 'that's just the price you have to be prepared to pay for fame.'

'You definitely seem prepared to make the sacrifice so I'm sure you'll make it,' I said sincerely and she looked pleased.

'I've been thinking lately that I want to work with animals,' I said, surprising myself more than Kylie.

She looked a bit sorry for me but she said kindly, 'Maybe you could do a cameo on some show on Animal Planet'.

Scott stared at me when he saw me and I wondered uneasily if I had a snotty nose from all the air conditioning, but then he said, 'Are you trying to be a smurf?' and I remembered my blue-streaked hair.

'It's a statement,' I told him helpfully.

'A statement of what?' he asked.

'I'm not sure,' I admitted.

He looked confused.

'Would Alicia have let you colour your hair?' he asked.

'Yes,' I said, 'I think so, if it washed out, and this one does.'

Over tacos that evening, when I told him about how Kylie wanted to be famous when she grows up, Scott said that there are many millions of Americans who don't want to be famous but everyone forgets that they exist because they're not on reality TV shows. Then it got a little awkward because he said that he hadn't been spying on me but he noticed because I borrowed his iPad that I seemed very interested in reading about death. He wanted me to go see a friend of a friend of his, called Dr Steve, who specialises in bereavement counselling for kids.

'I can't think of anything worse,' I said rudely. 'I've already been to Mrs Scanlon in Ireland and I'm therapied out,' I added.

Scott looked sympathetic.

'If you want to talk but you don't want to talk to me, you can try Joanna, or you can try Ben; he's an excellent listener and never judgemental.'

I nodded.

'I promise,' I said.

Chapter 6

Scott and Leela were heading for Jackson Hole, Wyoming, to attend the wedding of Scott's friend, Ethan, a dentist who had fallen in love with one of his patients.

'Do you know where Wyoming is, Evie?' Scott challenged on Friday morning as I ate a bowl of Lucky Charms.

I paused to think. I had been focusing on how a dentist could fall in love with someone while drilling her teeth.

'Sure,' I replied, I hoped with a degree of nonchalance. 'Wyoming is in Massachusetts.'

Scott clutched his stomach and faked mock hysterical laughter.

'Not even close, Evie, and Wyoming is a STATE!' he called out, as he disappeared down the corridor, returning a few minutes later with a large map of the United States, which he handed to me with a flourish.

'You can learn the states and their capitals. Pop quiz when I get back.'

Scott stared resignedly at Leela's three matching crocodile skin suitcases. 'We are only going to be away for two nights, Leela,' and turning to me, he muttered, 'and you, you're the person who gets offended when Americans think that Dublin is in Scotland.'

'Point taken,' I said and I took the map into my bedroom.

I knew the U.S. was a big country, obviously, but I had no idea it was so amazingly enormous. I guess I had been thinking of it as not extending beyond the Brooklyn Bridge. The population of the Republic of Ireland is about four and a half million and the population of the United States is more than three hundred million. I couldn't get my head around that number of people. We are just a pimple, I thought, compared to America.

Scott had roped Joanna into staying in the apartment all weekend to look after me.

'I don't need a babysitter,' I'd argued.

'Joanna might,' he said. 'Have fun!' And we did.

We spent Friday night eating limited edition blueberry cheesecake ice cream and playing a grand slam tennis tournament on Wii. We eventually had to put Ben in my room while we played because he was so excited by the sound of the Wii tennis ball that he kept driving himself (and us) crazy, running around, sniffing everywhere and making excited yelping noises in his hopeless quest to find the cyber ball.

On Saturday afternoon I helped Joanna stock the medicine shelves in the clinic and we chatted about all kinds of stuff.

'Where in Canada are you from?' I asked her.

'Prince Edward Island,' she answered.

'Prince Edward Island, are you serious?' I said, delighted. 'That's where *Anne of Green Gables* is from. It was one of

47

Mum's favourite books.'

She smiled.

'I am debt free, thanks to Anne with an 'e'.

'What do you mean?' I asked, intrigued.

'Well, I was nine years old, collecting shells on Cavendish beach, when a bunch of Japanese tourists swarmed all over me. They were so excited and kept pointing at me and snapping photographs and exclaiming, "Anne, Anne" because I suppose I looked like their image of *Anne of Green Gables*,' and she pointed wryly to her red hair. 'I told my mom about it and she's not the type of woman to miss out on a good business opportunity. She sewed some old-fashioned calico dresses for me, did up my hair in two braids and used a brown eyeliner pencil to paint some freckles on my face. Our house was on one of the main roads and she cajoled my father into building a little stand in front of it with a hand-painted sign saying, "Have your photograph taken with *Anne of Green Gables*." The tourists lapped it up.

'For the rest of that summer and every summer after that, I had a readymade job. I just sat on a little wooden stool in the stand and tourists paid to have their photographs taken with me. The European tourists often kissed me on the cheek, but we had to ban the kissing because they kept smudging my fake freckles so that it looked like I had mud smeared on my face. During the second summer, my mom and my sister started selling lemonade and snacks like hot dogs at the stand. My parents put all the *Anne* money into a college trust fund for me and the snacks money into an account for my sister.'

'Did you like being Anne?' I wondered.

'Most of the time, yes, but there were some downers. The *Anne of Green Gables* in the books did not wear glasses and I've always been too squeamish to wear contact lenses so I had to whip off my glasses whenever tourists stopped by, and that led to quite a few accidents, trust me. And the business fell off a lot when I got older. A seventeen-year-old squeezed into a child's dress with braids in her hair wasn't as popular with the tourists.'

'It started to get creepy.' Joanna giggled. 'And I had to put up with lots of flak from the dumb kids at school.'

'I can imagine,' I said sympathetically. 'Did it bother you a lot?'

She nodded, 'Yes, at the time, not that I let them know that.'

Then she added, 'But Evie, I promise you this, you will NEVER see me with my hair in braids.'

'Ok, Anne with an "e"!' I said and we both laughed until we heard a polite cough coming from the waiting room.

'I'll go see who it is.' And I skipped out to the waiting room.

It was Him, the boy with the Rangers cap. In his left hand he carried a cage with a large blue and green parrot with a curved beak.

'Hi!' he said. 'How is the messed-up turtle?'

'Fine, more than fine, totally good, his leg was broken and it's healing really well now,' I babbled.

'Good, glad he's doing ok. I know you guys close early

on Saturdays. I'm just looking for some beak conditioner,' he said.

Joanna breezed through the door and her face immediately broke into a wide smile.

'Hi! Finn, how are you doing? What's up with Kurt?'

But Kurt jumped in before Finn could answer.

'Booooreeeeeeed!' he interjected.

We all jumped.

'Sorry,' said Finn. 'Kurt's manners need a little work. I think his beak is overgrown again.'

'Let's take a look,' said Joanna and she picked up the cage as Finn and I followed her into the examining room.

Unluckily, the phone rang. I ran back and picked it up. It was that pompous old windbag, Adrienne Weismann, a woman with hair the colour of cigarette ash and the bane of Scott's existence. She currently has three cats, Muffles, Delilah and KitKat, and she is on her fourth husband. She wrote a book about a zillion years ago called *Kitty Tips; From One Cat Lover To Another*. She considers herself an expert in the field of feline veterinary medicine. By the time she has exhausted her homemade remedies on one of her sick cats and brings them in to Scott, it's usually far too late to help them. Then she acts like Scott killed her beloved pussies through his incompetence, but she still keeps coming back. Scott thinks her only joy in life is torturing him. It took me at least ten minutes to schedule an appointment for her to bring in Muffles and get her off the phone.

I ran to the examining room to see what was happening

with Kurt. I'd never come across a rude bird with a beak problem before. As I turned the corner and reached the step, I tripped so that I landed right inside the doorway, head first, on my knees.

'That's one way of making an entrance,' said Finn, reaching down and hauling me up like I was a sack of potatoes.

I glared at Ben. He not only had access to every bed in the roomy apartment upstairs but he was also the sole owner of his very own, comfortable, super soft, donut bed. And yet, he decides to take a mid-afternoon snooze on the step up to the examining room. Why didn't we just give him a key to the apartment, since he acted like he owns it! Ben yawned and he seemed to be laughing at me. With Finn and Joanna, that would make three then. I glared at Joanna as well. She's just as clumsy as I am so I didn't know what she had to laugh about.

Finn picked up Kurt's cage and stepped past me.

'Still booooored!' said Kurt.

'Shut up, Kurt!' said Finn, 'And say hello to, what's your name?'

'Evangeline,' I said, firmly, 'but everyone calls me Evie.'

'Say hello Evie,' Finn instructed.

'Hello, Evie, pleased to meet you,' responded Kurt promptly and he held out one of his claws through the bars of his cage for me to shake.

'My pleasure,' I responded and shook his claw gingerly. I didn't totally trust Kurt.

'Finn – that's an Irish name. Are your parents Irish?' I asked.

'Nope, not a drop of Irish blood as far as I know. My mom liked movies of Broadway musicals. Finn is her shorthand for *Finian's Rainbow*.'

'Oh, it's lucky she didn't call you Georg. You know, like Captain von Trapp from *The Sound of Music*,' I pointed out.

'Wow!' said Finn, 'you're pretty close to the mark. That honour was reserved for my little brother, but we call him Greg now.'

'Georg was way too cruel,' he added.

'I don't know about that,' said Joanna, 'I think "Georg" could be a cool name.'

Finn and I exchanged quick looks. 'Georg' could never be a cool name for anyone – boy, girl, straight, gay, nobody.

'No charge for the visit,' said Joanna, 'just three dollars for the beak conditioner.'

I was able to sneak a long look at Finn as he dug his wallet out of the back pocket of his jeans. I'd never met a boy who owned a wallet before. Finn's brown hair was a little long, just below his collar, and his eyes were dark and difficult to read. He had a dark shadow of stubble on his face and I wanted to reach up and touch it just to see what it felt like, but I didn't. Mum always told me to try to recognise the times when it is important to pretend to be normal, and this was one of them.

As Finn pulled some dollar bills out of his wallet, I noticed he was left-handed and that two, thin, white scars stood out on his deeply tanned left arm. He looked at me looking at him.

'Ice hockey,' he said, 'a contact sport.' He handed over the cash to Joanna.

'Bye, enjoy the rest of the weekend,' she said, and Finn trooped out, carrying Kurt in his cage.

'Tell someone who cares!' screeched Kurt.

'How old do you think Finn is?' I asked Joanna casually when the coast was clear.

She looked at me with a little teasing smile, which I ignored.

'I don't know,' she said, 'but I would guess sixteen.'

'Way too old for you to be friends with,' she added unnecessarily.

Scott and Leela returned from Wyoming the following evening and we ate Thai food together. As I was telling Scott about Kurt and Finn, Leela suddenly waved her chopsticks in the air, nearly taking one of Scott's eyes out.

'Finn WINTERS!' she announced triumphantly. 'I know about him. My law firm represented his mother in the divorce. Well, we did represent her until she stopped being able to pay our fees and then we dumped her!' She moistened her lips before continuing.

'Finn's father is an eminent Park Avenue psychiatrist and his mother is a theatre producer. They had a very long, very expensive, nasty divorce, with the two boys caught right in the middle of a big custody battle and …'

Scott interrupted her abruptly.

'I don't think we want to hear gossip about your clients' private affairs. Don't lawyers have duties of confidentiality?'

Leela tossed her head, sending a long, stray, dark hair into my lemongrass soup.

I stared at it.

'Please, honey,' she snapped impatiently, 'where would the tabloids that you read get their information from without the divorce lawyers? The case was the usual mess: the parents fighting, the lawyers fighting and filling their cash registers and the judge kept changing her decisions, giving the kids to the dad in one decision, then to the mom, then handing them back to the dad. Anyway, that kid, Finn, took matters into his own hands. He ran away on New Year's Eve, taking the younger brother with him.'

'Ran away,' I gasped, forgetting about the hair slithering in my soup. 'How old was he?'

'Let me think. He must be fourteen now and the little brother, Craig or Greg, or something like that, is twelve,' said Leela.

'I thought Finn was at least sixteen,' I said.

Leela continued, 'Guess where the boys turned up?'

Scott and I remained silent.

'WISCONSIN. They were living in a trailer home and Finn managed to talk himself into some job as an assistant to a mechanic in a garage. Apparently, some customer at the garage got suspicious and called the police who brought the boys back.'

'What happened then?' I asked, fascinated.

'The parents were so shook up that they decided to stop the divorce litigation and fire all the lawyers. They mediated an agreement and now the boys live fifty percent of the time with the mom and the other half with the dad. The mom still owes our firm money, though.'

But I had stopped listening. I had retreated deep inside my own head, thinking about a runaway. I would have been way too scared to do something like that.

Chapter 7

Kylie and I hung out in my room this morning. We were listening to a new singer on Scott's iPad who had a name that sounded like a breakfast cereal.

'She is my fashion inspiration,' Kylie confided, as she wandered around my room, looking at my stuff. I admired the purple and orange streaks in her hair.

'What's this?' she asked, picking up a shiny mahogany box and trying to open the lid, but it was locked.

'It's nothing,' I said. 'Just some stuff my mum put in there for me to open when I turn sixteen.'

'Exciting!' she exclaimed. 'It's like a movie. What kind of stuff do you think is in there?'

I felt embarrassed.

'I'm not sure,' I said. 'Stuff about my dad, maybe, I never met him.'

'Do you wonder about your dad?' she asked.

'No,' I said. 'I did when I was little,' I added, to be totally honest.

'Do you ever think he will turn up one day looking for you?' she asked.

I shook my head. 'No way. Only Mum believed that. She

was a hopeless romantic. Well, that's what her friends said about her, but not in a mean way, just in a "that's Alicia, that's who she is" exasperated but accepting sort of way.'

'Do you ever wonder about your biological parents in China?' I asked.

'Not really,' she said and we both laughed. 'But I go to this club once a month. It's for adopted kids in Manhattan. There are so many of us. We talk about stuff but mostly we go on outings to museums and the Bronx Zoo and kayaking in the Catskills.'

'What kind of stuff do you guys talk about?' I asked.

Kylie shrugged.

'Things. Like how annoying it is when some people find it hard to accept that an Asian kid has a white mom, that kind of thing. Remember last week when we were in Dylan's Candy Bar and the woman in the ugliest jeans ever asked me where I was from and I said, "Here, New York" and she said, "No, I mean where are you *really* from?"'

Suddenly Kylie leaned over and touched the mute sign on the iPad.

'What is that weird noise?' she asked. It was coming from under my bed. I got down on my knees to investigate. I found Ben having a snooze and snoring happily.

'That's so cute,' said Kylie.

'How come it's so cute when dogs snore but not cute at all when humans do?'

I didn't know, but she was right. Eurdes barged into the room without knocking and I was kind of glad that she was

57

fully dressed, what with Kylie being there and all.

'Dr Brooks is going to visit a pig and he wants to know if you and your friend want to go with him,' she announced.

'A pig, Eurdes? Are you sure he said *pig*?'

'I can understand English, you know,' she said, huffily. 'That's what he said, a pig, and I'm not paid to be a messenger.'

'I'm sorry, Eurdes. I wasn't doubting your English. I just didn't think there were any pigs in the city.'

'Huh, pigs, New York is full of them,' and she snorted with laughter at her own joke.

'Come on, let's go!' I said, hustling Kylie out of the door.

Ray's apartment was in the East Village. He is a tall guy, around Scott's age, with longish dark hair. He answered the door wearing a faded Snoopy t-shirt and orange flip-flops, revealing very long and crusty toenails. Kylie told me Ray is a hipster, which is a dying breed. In his apartment he had about six computers, all switched on. We trooped in single file behind him as he led us through to the back door.

'Sorry about the mess. I don't clean when I'm working, when I'm in the zone. You have to drop everything when the creative juices are pumping.'

'I'm an animator,' he added, looking at myself and Kylie. 'I was almost part of a team that was nominated for a Golden Globe for Best Animated Feature last year.'

'Cool!' said Kylie. 'What movies have you made? *Toy Story*?

'No.'

'*Cars?*'

'No.'

'*Gnomeo and Juliet?*'

'No.'

I had a try.

'*The Fantastic Mr Fox?* That's my favourite,' I added.

'No,' said Ray, sounding a little peeved, 'but I did an oat-meal commercial with animated bears. I'll show it to you guys after the doc has looked at Arnold.'

For Kylie, Ray's star factor had started to fade.

Scott had treated Arnold before and had told us about him during the car trip to Ray's apartment.

'He's a miniature pot-bellied pig.'

'Oh, a little pig, how sweet,' said Kylie.

'*Miniature* is relative,' grinned Scott. 'He weighs about a hundred and thirty pounds.'

'Why would anyone keep a pig as a pet?' I wondered.

'Pigs are very intelligent and affectionate, and very clean,' said Scott.

'Don't they smell bad?' I asked.

'Nope. That's a myth. Arnold is about seven years old. He's very good at opening things with his snout. The last time Ray called me, Arnold had learned to open the refrigerator and had gorged himself on everything in there, which was mainly old pizza. I think Ray got him at first just because he thought it would be "cool" to have a pet pig. But he didn't turn around and abandon him like so many other people do when the novelty wears off. He's pretty attached to that pig.'

'What's wrong with Arnold?' asked Kylie.

'Nothing. He needs a vaccination. It's just one little shot.'

Ray opened the glass sliding doors to the long, narrow, concrete backyard. I thought Arnold would be pink but he was black. We could see him rooting through a soft mound of dirt at the far end of the yard. Scott told us to wait by the glass doors in front of the fence, which looked like it had been hammed together out of parts of Ikea furniture and painted white.

Scott took out his needle, filled it, scaled the fence and walked steadily towards the back of the yard. Arnold glanced up, saw Scott, didn't like what he saw and charged. I don't think I've ever seen anyone move so fast. Scott made it back over the fence in three seconds flat. It's pretty frightening when a wheelbarrow-sized portion of pork is pounding towards you.

'Arnie, STOP!' yelled Ray, and Arnold halted in his tracks.

'Sit!' commanded Ray, and Arnold sat, just like a well-trained dog.

Ray smiled with pride and fondness as he put a leash on the pig.

'You can give it to him now, Dr Brooks,' he said.

Scott didn't waste time in giving Arnold the injection. Then he waved at us to come through the gate. Arnold rolled over for a belly rub and we obliged. His belly was soft but his back was hard and dense and there was a hairy Mohawk running along it.

'You have great hair, Dr Brooks,' said Kylie. 'It didn't even get ruined when you were sprinting away from Arnold.'

Scott looked at Kylie as if she had just teleported herself from Jupiter.

'Thank you,' he said.

'You're welcome,' Kylie replied.

'I'm thinking of getting another pig as a companion to Arnie,' Ray said.

'Pigs are very social creatures. I think Arnold would like that,' Scott said, obviously relieved to move the subject away from his hair. 'But you need more space.'

Then we went inside to watch the forty-five second animated bears oatmeal commercial on Ray's computer, three times in a row, with Ray chuckling softly each time and humming the jingle as we watched. Scott intervened when Ray started to replay the commercial a fourth time.

'Sorry, we have to go. Diesel, a pet white rat with a toothache, is waiting for us back at the clinic.'

Ray looked disappointed.

'A rat, so gross!' said Kylie. 'Can you drop me off at Mom's gallery on the way home?'

'Sure,' replied Scott.

'Guys, talking of rats, I was nearly on the team that did the animation for the *Ratatouille* movie,' said Ray.

We all stared at him.

'That's cool, Ray,' said Scott.

Ray smiled and gave Kylie and me a disk, which he explained had more examples of his work.

'Thank you,' we said in unison.

As we drove up Third Avenue, I asked, 'Scott, could I please have a pot-bellied pig for my birthday next February, or for Christmas, that's even sooner?'

'You can take some time to think about it,' I suggested generously.

Scott snorted.

'I don't need time, thanks. NO WAY to a pig. We don't have the outdoor space and anyway, aren't you going back to Ireland in September? So you won't be here to take care of him.'

'Yes, of course I'm going back,' I said.

Scott didn't look upset at all.

'Oh, I didn't know you were going back to Ireland,' said Kylie. 'That stinks!'

At least someone would miss me, I thought sulkily.

Chapter 8

The rest of the week dragged. Every day it got hotter and more humid. Frank said to me, 'You wait until August, Irish. Then you'll see what sticky heat is like.'

On Friday, Kylie called to say that she and her mom had plans to stay with family at their summer home in the Berkshires for the weekend. The Berkshires are mountains about a four-hour drive away. Kylie's grandparents' house is on a wooded hill above a big lake where Kylie swims and goes boating with her cousins. It sounded like a lot of fun.

On Saturday, I had a Big Fight with Scott. We were stocking up the dog and cat food on the shelves downstairs late in the afternoon. The AC wasn't working properly and it was way too hot and I missed Ireland and I missed Mum. Scott kept trying to tease me out of my grumpy mood, which only made me grumpier.

Then he got all quiet and said softly, 'I know you are missing your mom a lot. I miss her too.'

I flipped out.

'You don't know anything. For starters, I'm not missing MOM a lot. She wasn't my MOM. I'm from Ireland; we don't say 'MOM' there. That's a dumb word for dumb Americans. And, what are you talking about? You COULDN'T possibly be missing her. You hardly ever saw her. She didn't even know you anymore.'

I threw down the can of Paul Newman's dog food and climbed the spiral staircase to the apartment; half-walked, half-ran into my room and banged the door shut very hard. I threw the stupid Lisa Simpson cover off my bed and just lay on top of the sheets.

Ben started crying outside the door, a very irritating, high-pitched, whining, 'ooooh' 'oooh' 'oooh'. I had to get up to let him in. He jumped up on the bed and rolled over with his four paws waving in the air, waiting for a belly rub. Ben can be a bit self- absorbed. I rubbed his belly and he licked my hand and then my face. His tongue is harsh and he definitely doesn't have the best-smelling breath in the world.

I felt sorry for myself for being an orphan, although technically I may not be an orphan at all. It's a bit complicated, but basically Mum fell madly in love with an Irish guy, the lead guitarist in a band from Galway in the West of Ireland. At that time, Mum was in her first year of drama school in New York City. When she saw my dad strutting his stuff in the Mercury Lounge, a bar in the East Village, it was love at first guitar chord. My dad was not a rich, famous rock star, although when I was little, I sometimes pretended he was.

My parents were both eighteen when they met. Mum dropped drama school and left all her friends and family in America to follow my dad back to Ireland. They lived together for a few months in a grotty bedsit in Ranelagh in

Dublin. When Mum got pregnant with me, my dad couldn't handle it. He jumped ship and went to Australia, we think, and Mum never heard from him again. Janet sometimes said that, with his kind of character, we were probably lucky my dad didn't hang around. Mum never answered. She never said a bad word about my dad. She didn't go back to America. She believed my dad would come back one day. I did not – except when I was very little.

Mum became an actress, mainly in the theatre, but now and again TV work cropped up. My favourite commercial was the one for cottage cheese. I mean, Mum was good in it; cottage cheese is disgusting.

After playing Jack in *Jack and the Beanstalk* at the Gaiety Theatre in Dublin, she had a major part in a TV crime series, set in Putney in London. She played an American forensic investigator named Carolyn Morrison, who always wore tiny miniskirts regardless of the weather. She helped the main character, Detective Grenfell, as he tried to solve a serial murder case. However, the murderer strangled Mum in the toilet of a pub. This took place in the last episode of the first season, right after Detective Grenfell realised he had fallen in love with her. It was a real shame because we had been hoping very hard that Mum would be kept on for another season.

After being unnecessarily killed off, Mum performed in quite a few plays in Dublin, Belfast, London and Edinburgh and also in lots of small, dead, miserable towns up and down the coast of England. Once, she had a part for nine weeks in a farce in Paris and we had a brilliant time except for the fact that she never got paid for the last three weeks. The following winter, we were stuck in the Isle of Man for a month, a crushingly boring experience for both of us.

However, about two years ago, when I had just turned ten, Mum decided to settle down and stay put in Dublin. I suspect that she did this for my sake because I hated changing schools so often. When you are the new kid, everyone stares at you and asks loads of questions. The first question they always ask is, 'Where are you from?' But when I answered, 'Dublin' they usually made fun of me and said I didn't sound like I was from Dublin at all and I wasn't really Irish. Birmingham was the worst. On my first day, a girl called Vivienne, with dyed plum hair, said that I was a mongrel. I told her that was fine with me so long as I didn't have plum hair. Now, after over two years straight of living in Dublin, I am no longer from nowhere. I am Irish. I can even speak Irish pretty well, although it's not nearly my best subject.

Mum worked as the front-of-house manager at the Abbey Theatre in Dublin. That job sounds a good bit grander than it actually was. But it was fun to hang around the theatre in the evenings. An actor called Brendan Byrne was in a play last year, called *The Playboy of the Western World*. When the run finished, Mr Byrne called me into his dressing room and presented me with a gigantic, unbelievably soft, pale blue elephant, which I christened Ellie. I was too old for a toy like that but it was really great of him.

I wasn't massively sorry when the play finished because

Mum had developed a bit of a crush on him. I knew she definitely had a crush because she kept forgetting to put the meat in the spaghetti bolognaise, that kind of thing. I wished she were here now, cooking spaghetti and forgetting the mince or brushing the knots out of my hair, which she did most mornings, and we chatted away the whole time. She used to come up with these fun ways to spend Mondays, which were her days off and, sometimes, she even let me miss school so we could go on adventures together. 'Misadventures,' Janet called them.

I thought about Mum's funeral. The wake took place in Mum's friend David's house in Drumcondra because our flat on North Great George's Street was way too small. David inherited the house on Griffith Avenue from his parents. It is a beautiful wide road lined with trees. David's house is very large and grand and elegant, with bay windows and Victorian antique furniture and Persian rugs.

The entire theatre community in Dublin turned out and loads of artsy types from London as well and there were three Scots in their kilts and knee-high socks who did a play with Mum at the Edinburgh festival a few years ago. All day long, people kissed me and shook my hand and patted my hair and offered me toasted ham and cheese sandwiches and olives and smoked salmon on brown bread and miniature Mars bars and cans of Coke. I must have drunk about five cans of Coke that day.

All of the kids from my class at school came, wearing their school uniforms even though it was Saturday. John Donaghy came up to me and touched me on my right elbow and said, 'Sorry about your mum,' in a low voice. That was probably the only time I was not interested in seeing him, so I just said, 'That's ok, thanks'. He stood beside me awkwardly for a few minutes and then he left, taking a can of Coke and two bags of salt and vinegar Tayto crisps from the kitchen counter with him.

Mrs Scanlon turned up, looking a bit lost and wearing wide black trousers instead of her usual gypsy skirt, but I ducked behind people or furniture whenever I noticed her searching for me.

There was a lot of talking going on, either whispering very loudly (that's called a stage whisper), or speaking in fake cheerful voices, or else they were crying. But my eyes were dry and itchy all day. I wore a new dress from Brown Thomas's – navy with polka dots, accessorised with scratchy, bright red wool tights. Mum hated black. Scott wore a very sharp, black Hugo Boss suit with a thin black tie and he hung out beside me most of the time, but we hardly talked at all.

Some of the drama students from Trinity College who knew Mum because she occasionally taught them, set up a small stage made out of banana crates and performed a few scenes between Beatrice and Benedick from *Much Ado About Nothing* because that was Mum's favourite play. Although the students were funny, especially Aileen, who played Beatrice, nobody laughed except for a tall, skinny man with a horrible, wispy goatee that nobody knew. I think all the normal people felt uncomfortable about laughing at a funeral, so the play flopped. The students should have performed a tragedy.

Some singing and music started up after the play – traditional, sad, Irish ballads about hungry children and fishermen lost at sea, lonely emigrants in Boston, writing letters to their families left behind, and failed but glorious rebellions against the English. Janet has a beautiful, sweet voice. People say it is like an Irish linnet, which may or may not be true. I don't know because I've never heard an Irish linnet and I bet they haven't either.

As the music started to wind down, David clapped his hands for silence. He fiddled with the iPod docking station for a moment, while we all waited. Then the opening guitar chords of *Haunted* by Shane MacGowan and Sinead O'Connor filled the room. The song lasted nearly four minutes and it was the only time during that day that I didn't feel like a dinosaur fossil enclosed in a glacier of ice for millions and millions of years. Mum loved that song so much. We sang it all the time, and I mean ALL THE TIME. Nearly everyone joined in singing the chorus and we butchered it but we didn't care. When we finished singing, the atmosphere in the house seemed lighter, almost giddy. I wished Mum could have been there. She loved a party.

I felt Ben prodding me with his right paw, demanding attention, and memories of the funeral vanished. I didn't feel angry anymore, but I started to feel slightly sick in my stomach about being mean to Scott. I was tired of thinking. I wish there was a course of antibiotics you could take to stop THINKING, not forever, of course, but just to have a break once in a while.

I also began to get hungry and started fantasising about the leftover pizza in the refrigerator. But I felt weird about going out to the kitchen. I had a terrible feeling that I had acted like a whiny brat. It was not a comfortable feeling.

When it had turned completely dark outside and I could no longer hear the sounds of the visitors leaving the History Museum, Scott knocked on my door and said, 'Can I come in, Evie?'

I said, 'Ok, sure!' but it didn't come out as clearly and casually as I had meant it to.

Scott walked in and pushed Ben over a little so he had room to sit beside me on the bed.

'Evie,' he began, 'if there is anything I could change, it would have been, I mean, I wish I had spent so much more time with you and your mom. Damn it, sorry, I mean your *mum*. I wish I had been there for you guys. I should have been there.'

I felt even guiltier. When you have behaved badly but the person you were mean to is all nice and gentle, it makes you feel a lot worse. Scott continued, running his hand quickly through his hair so that it stood on the top of his head in spikes, 'I am clueless about all this. I don't know anything about kids. I'm screwing it all up.'

'No, no, you're not!' I said quickly. 'You *do* know about kids. You were a kid once. And Joanna said only last week that you are still just a big kid.'

I realised immediately that I had been tactless so I rushed ahead.

'I am very, very sorry for calling you a dumb American. You are not a dumb American. You're just American.'

And he said, 'Thank you, I think.'

Ben crawled up between us.

'What about if we try and figure things out together as we go along? What do you say?' said Scott.

'Ok, sure, we can do that. Easy peasy!' I said.

Neither of us said anything more for a few minutes. But it was not a strained silence. There was no tension at all. We both just kept stroking Ben and scratching his ears and he was enjoying the attention enormously.

Eventually, Scott said, 'I know you know this, but it is ok to cry sometimes. Crying does not make you a crybaby. Look at Ben, he cries all the time.'

I lost my ability to cry when Mum died, which is bizarre because I was often in floods of tears before over stupid little things. I cried up a storm when Mum wouldn't let me spend the bank holiday Easter weekend with my friend Deirdre and her family at her grandfather's house on the Aran Islands. Now, my eyes often get sore and itchy, but no water comes out. I didn't want to say anything to Scott about my inability to cry. I had a sneaky suspicion that he might not like me. I mean, what kind of weird kid does not cry when their mother dies?

So, I just said, 'Yeah, I know. I'm ok. I don't feel like blubbing right this minute.'

Scott patted me clumsily on my head like I was a pet, but I didn't mind. We gave Ben a Scooby snack for being an empathy dog. Then we watched an episode of *The Dog Whisperer* by unanimous vote. Scott had to help Ben cast his vote because he tends to lift his left front paw for all choices when you ask him. I think that's partly because he's such an eager-to-please kind of dog.

Chapter 9

It's hard to believe that I've been in New York for over a month already. This morning, I went to Zabars to get some juicy bones for Ben. Zabars is a very cool delicatessen on Broadway, a few blocks from Scott's apartment. They sell all kinds of delicious food but you have to cope with a horde of tiny, wrinkled old ladies that deliberately knock into your knees with their mini-trolleys. Scott says that Zabars should hand out shin guards when you walk in the door.

Joanna thinks Ben is named in honour of Benjamin Franklin and she teases Scott about that because we get so many dogs and cats in the clinic named after American Presidents. We treated three dogs called Lincoln last week and two cats called Obama the week before. Scott is crazy about Benjamin Franklin and he has a marble bust of him in his room. I asked Scott if he named Ben after his hero but he said, 'absolutely not', that he just named Ben 'Ben' because it is a strong, one-syllable word, which was easy for a puppy to get used to. Scott gave me a book about Benjamin Franklin. The more I learn about Benjamin Franklin, the less I think Ben was named after him. Benjamin Franklin was very smart.

Even Scott concedes that Ben is not the brightest dog in the world, just bright enough. But, of course, we would never hurt Ben's feelings by letting him hear that and we wouldn't take kindly to someone else saying it either.

It was Eurdes's day today. She's from Brazil but she doesn't speak Brazilian because Scott explained to me that there is no such language. She speaks Portuguese because, hundreds of years ago, the Portuguese invaded Brazil and stayed. They killed a lot of the native people in horrible ways. They brought European diseases with them that killed even more of the native people. Eurdes doesn't seem interested in her country's bloody past. This surprised me because in Ireland we are obsessed with our history, so much so that people try to change it all the time.

Back in March, right before St Paddy's Day, I found myself in serious trouble at school for throwing Andrew Toohey's metal Batman pencil case at Cian Tiernan's head. I completely lost the plot when Cian slagged off Michael Collins, who is my 'Person I Most Admire' (Not Including Blood Relatives). Michael Collins was a great leader in the Irish War of Independence. He's practically the Irish George Washington, not that someone like Cian appreciates how great he was. He said that his dad said that Michael Collins was massively overrated. Not satisfied with slagging off my number one Irish patriot, Cian threw in a nasty dig at Mum as well, saying that his mum said my mum shouldn't be collecting the Children's Allowance because she was American and that meant I was American as well and we were sponging off the state. It was very unlucky that Andrew's pencil case was right next to my hand, especially because most of the kids in my class had soft, plastic pencil cases. But anyway, it barely touched Cian, just grazed the side of his head. It wasn't very manly of him to squeal on me. I was suspended for three days without even getting the opportunity to tell my side of the story. The principal, Mr Smyth, said that it did not matter what provocation I had received; violence could never be justified. I thought about telling him that violence against the Nazis was justified, but I knew that would be cheeky and I was in enough trouble already.

Both Mr and Mrs Tiernan turned up uninvited at our flat that night, which was very unpleasant because I hadn't mentioned my suspension to Mum and I had binned the note from Mr Smyth that I was supposed to give to her. To be fair to me, I did that to try to avoid worrying her, which was working out well until the Tiernans ruined it.

Mrs Tiernan told Mum that I was a hooligan and that she had a good mind to have the police press charges because I belonged in Mountjoy Prison. Mr Tiernan looked very uncomfortable and sweaty and said that that was going too far. Way too far, in my opinion.

After Mum calmed the Tiernans down and sent them on their way, she said to me, 'You know better than that. You have to use your words.'

I said, 'Sorry, Mum, for letting you down.'

She responded, 'You let yourself down.'

She topped that with, 'I'm very disappointed in you.'

Mum made me stay alone in my room without TV or any books or her laptop or other distractions so that I could think about my actions. She occasionally brought me trays of my least favourite food, like Shepherd's Pie. It was like being in jail except I was not permitted to make the one phone call, which anyone who has ever watched TV knows I was entitled to.

I did come to regret what I did. I could have caused Cian brain damage, or rather, *more* brain damage because he seemed to have suffered some already. I could even have killed him. I tried hard to think about Cian's good qualities. That took up most of my time. Eventually, I remembered that he was very generous about sharing his crisps at lunchtime. He always offered them around straight away as soon as he opened the bag. He didn't wait until the bag was nearly empty and there were only teeny, bitty crisps left at the bottom, like some other kids did.

I felt genuine remorse about my attempted murder. So, I had no problem apologising to him when I went back to school, but it still rankles that he never apologised to me. If it were not for Michael Collins and other brave Irish men and women, Ireland would still be a little British colony and the Tiernans would be nothing but indentured servants. I am not entirely sure what 'indentured' means but it sounds right.

Chapter 10

Scott took me with him up to the Bronx yesterday to visit a lame horse at the Riverside stables in Van Cortlandt Park. Through the open doors of the inside arena, we watched a mothers' and daughters' group having a riding lesson.

'Oh no!' groaned Scott. 'I think that woman on the chestnut mare is Christina Morgan, one of my more committed stalkers. I don't know why I am such a magnet for bored divorcees.'

'Joanna says it might have something to do with your James Bond complex,' I replied.

'That's a compliment,' Scott said cheerfully.

'I don't think anything with the word "complex" in it is a compliment. And maybe if you didn't always look like you stepped off the cover of GQ magazine, you would have less worries about stalkers.'

'GQ!' said Scott with a low whistle. 'Not bad. I can't help knowing how to dress, and I buy the GQs for the clients!'

My mouth dropped open.

'Yeah, sure, the people who come into the clinic, like Mr Fannelli, are *so* GQ readers.'

Scott pulled off his brown aviator sunglasses and squinted as he peered closer at the riders.

'It's not Christina,' he said with relief, 'just some woman who must visit the same hairdresser for her extensions. Let's go find this lame horse.'

One of the grooms led us into the stalls, explaining that the horse had just arrived that morning and he had noticed she was lame. He suspected laminitis. I had never seen a real horse up close before. One time in Dingle, when I was a little kid, I had a ride on a very sweet white donkey called Noddy. But the nearest I have been to a horse was the plastic contraption masquerading as a horse in the play *War Horse* that Mum's friend, David produced in a theatre in Belfast last autumn.

The groom led a mare, Bobbi, out of her stall. She was dapple grey with a black mane and markings from her hooves to half way up her knees that looked like black socks. I patted her gently on her neck and she nuzzled her face into me. I inhaled the smell – the intensely warm, comforting, sweetish smell of horse and hay feed. Almost instantaneously, I felt the *Joy To The World sha la la la* feeling, except it was a quieter, calmer, feeling, like lowercase *joy to the world* and minus the *sha la la la* bit.

Looking up from the hoof he was examining, Scott half smiled and half-laughed at me.

'You get it, Evie. I knew you would. People get horses or they don't. There are no in-betweens.'

I nodded slowly. I get it. At least, I think I get it.

'Will she be ok?' I asked anxiously.

Scott straightened up.

'It is laminitis but we have caught it early. She should be ok after a few months.'

As he discussed treatment with the groom, I patted Bobbi on her face and scratched her ears, talking soothing nonsense with her. She seemed to like it.

'Would you like to start riding lessons, Evie?' Scott asked.

I swung around.

'WOULD I? Yes, yes, yes, I would LOVE it!' I said, doing a little half-jump, half-skip.

'Ok, we'll get you started. They have classes for beginners on Sunday mornings.'

'But won't it be way too expensive?' I asked, worried.

Scott shook his head.

'Not a problem. Don't worry about it,' and he showed me how to lead Bobbi back into her stall, with my right hand on the halter just below her neck and my left hand further down on the lead rope.

Back at the clinic, concerned owners and their pets took up every spare centimetre of space in the waiting room.

'Dudley is first,' said Karen, our new, part-time receptionist.

'Hey!' said a bald man in a short-sleeved Hawaiian shirt, walking up to the reception desk and waving his thick, muscular, hairy arms in Karen's face. 'What is going on here? I was here first.'

Karen eyed him coolly.

'Except for appointments, we basically operate on a first-come first-served basis, but we have to see animals with a potentially critical or emergency condition first.'

'My pet is in a critical condition,' he complained.

Karen looked at him disbelievingly.

'Your cat has a *skin* infection,' she pointed out, loudly enough for everyone in the waiting room to hear. 'While we, of course, take that very seriously, it is not something we would classify as requiring immediate or emergency assistance. The sooner you return to your seat, the sooner we will be able to move things along.'

The bald man stood his ground.

'I am a very busy man. I don't have the time to waste half a day here. What is it going to cost to get me bumped up?' he said, pulling out a brown leather wallet.

Karen scribbled something on a card and handed it to him.

'What is this?' he asked.

'It's the address of the nearest vet, if you would like to go there.'

'You can catch a cab right outside the door,' she added.

The man slapped the white card back down on the reception desk and returned to his seat, muttering under his breath about 'lousy service'. Karen winked at me and I smiled at her before heading into the examining room.

First up was Dudley, a ten-month old beagle puppy that had somehow managed to eat a packet of disposable lady razors. It was all the more bizarre considering that his owner, Mr Graham, is a ninety-one year old widower. He offered no explanation and Scott asked for none. Second, we had an unidentifiable mutt who chased and caught her own tail, managing to break it. Next up, the bald Hawaiian shirt guy with his mangy cat and mangier attitude. He complained to Scott, 'You should fire your receptionist, she has an attitude.'

Scott sighed. It had been a long morning.

'Do I come around to your home uninvited and say you should fire your wife?' Scott asked and, without waiting for an answer, added, 'No, I don't! If you don't like my people, go somewhere else. Now, make up your mind, do you want me to treat your cat or not?'

The bald man looked sheepish. He said, 'Sorry, I'm having a rough day and I'm more worried about my cat than I care to admit.'

Now it was Scott's turn to look sheepish.

'No need to apologise for loving your cat. Let's get him up on the table and sort out his problem.'

Finally, after the bald man and his cat left, I watched Scott vaccinate an adorable litter of striped kittens.

'Who have we got next?' Scott asked Karen on the intercom, pulling off his latex gloves.

'Greg Winters with his rabbit, Dr Pepper.'

In strolled a kid about my own age with a tall man with black hair streaked with silver, and silver rectangular-framed glasses. The man greeted Scott, and, taking *The New York Times* out of his briefcase said that he would wait in the waiting room. He didn't look like a psychiatrist, I thought, and he has much better dress sense than my old psychologist,

Mrs Scanlon. I shut the door to the waiting room behind me.

'How have you been doing, Greg?' Scott inquired.

'Great, apart from my mosquito bites!' said Greg and I noticed a bunch of swollen red hives on his legs.

'And how about Finn?' Scott asked.

'He's good too.'

Greg didn't look very like his brother. Greg has sandy brown hair brushed forward and green eyes and a dimple in his left check, which is wasted on a boy. He is very cute in a could-be-in-a-boy-band kind of way. Finn's hair and eyes are dark and he looks like the type of boy who makes fun of boy bands.

'Hi, I'm Evie,' I said, holding out my hand, forgetting that the kids in New York don't shake hands, but Greg didn't seem to mind.

He shook my hand anyway.

'I know,' he said. 'You're the one that took on the bully dirt bags in the park, three to one, right?'

'What's that?' asked Scott.

'Nothing,' I said hastily and I smiled meaningfully at Greg who got the point straight away.

'What's up with Dr Pepper?' Scott asked.

Greg hesitated.

'He's not really sick. He hasn't been throwing up or anything but he seems to be itchy.'

'Rabbits actually can't throw up,' Scott said.

'Wow,' I said, 'lucky rabbits! I hate the feeling of puking.'

Scott and Greg lifted Dr Pepper out of his cage.

'Why did you get a rabbit?' I asked as Scott began to examine Dr Pepper.

Greg grinned.

'My Dad's a shrink and he had one of his shrink theories that it would be good for Finn and me to have pets while he and Mom got divorced. We both really wanted a dog, a Rhodesian ridgeback, but neither of our parents wanted the hassle of a dog, so they bought us a parrot and a rabbit instead. I was so mad at first; when you want a dog, a dumb bunny rabbit doesn't really cut it. But when I got to know Dr Pepper, I realised he has this amazing personality.'

I glanced at the black rabbit sitting motionless on the table except for an occasional scratch. He didn't seem to be brimming with charisma.

'My sister, Alicia, that's Evie's mom, had a pet rabbit when we were kids,' said Scott. 'He was called Tiger and he used to follow her around like a dog. Alicia brought him to visit me one weekend at college and he became a mascot for our hockey team.'

'Ice or field?' Greg asked.

'Definitely ice,' said Scott.

'I play with the Rangers Youth League,' said Greg. 'I can't wait for it to start up again in the fall.'

'Can girls play?' I wondered.

'Sure!' said Greg. 'Can you skate?'

'I can roller-skate, but I've never been ice-skating,' I answered.

'A bunch of us play at the rink at Chelsea Piers during the

summer. You should come with us sometime.'

'Ok, thanks,' I said.

'I'll hunt out my old boots,' said Scott, although he had not been invited.

'Back to Dr Pepper. Have you taken him anywhere different lately?' Scott quizzed Greg.

'I brought him to a kids' pet show and competition in Westchester at the weekend. A pet snail took first prize. Beaten by a stupid pet snail! That's not even a real pet.'

Greg looked astounded.

'Dr Pepper didn't walk away with the prize but he did pick up something – fur mites,' Scott explained. 'I'll put some flea powder on him and give you some more. You can dust him with it again in ten days, so we can be sure they are gone.'

'Thanks, Dr Brooks,' Greg said, glancing affectionately at Dr Pepper, still scratching and wrinkling his nose.

I could swear Dr Pepper winked at me.

'Did you see that?' I said.

'See what?' asked Scott and Greg at the same time.

'Nothing.'

I scratched Dr Pepper's ears.

'He's growing on me,' I said and Greg smiled.

Chapter 11

I had a crappy day. It started off okay, with the sun peeping in my bedroom window and the sounds of Scott singing badly while making French toast in the kitchen. Then I heard voices and I knew Leela must be with him. Usually when she stays over, she's gone before I get up as she's always going to meetings called breakfast networking. I had forgotten today was Saturday.

'Come and get it!' Scott yelled.

I sighed and reluctantly pulled on the green and purple kimono robe Kylie had given me because she is too tall for it now, and sauntered into the kitchen.

Scott and I had planned to go the beach on Fire Island today. We were going to drive to the ferry, taking Ben and some pastrami on rye sandwiches from Zabars. I hoped fervently that Leela did not plan to join us. She hates sand, I reminded myself.

As I drizzled syrup over my French toast, Scott's cell phone rang. It was his best friend, Jake, suggesting a spontaneous game of golf.

'Can't do it,' said Scott, 'Evie and I are heading to the beach.'

Leela intervened.

'Why don't you go play golf with Jake, sweetheart?' she said. 'You haven't seen him in ages. I want to treat Evie to a girl's day, a manicure and a nice lunch.'

I nearly yakked up a piece of my French toast.

Scott said, 'Thanks, Leela, but I think Evie has her heart set on the beach.'

Leela looked meaningfully at me. I hated her but she was right. Scott hardly ever got time to hang out with Jake.

'No, that's ok,' I said. 'We can go the beach another time. I'll go with Leela.'

'Are you sure?' asked Scott.

'Totally,' I said.

'I'll see you in fifteen minutes,' he told Jake.

After hanging up, he said, 'Thanks, Leela, very sweet of you,' and he gave her a long, lingering kiss on the mouth. I had no French toast left or I definitely would have choked.

I never had a manicure before and I was embarrassed to hold out my rather grubby little nails. I don't bite them but they don't appear to be interested in growing. But Jordan, the Filipino guy who filed my nails, was very easy to talk to. He told me that he wants to be a comedian on a TV show called *Saturday Night Live* and he is taking improvisation classes at night. He suggested that I choose a pale pink colour for my nails called 'Ballet Slippers', but I picked a blueish colour called 'Midnight Destiny'. Then I just flipped through magazines, waiting for Leela to finish. She went into the waxing room for a very long time. I heard her say she wanted her lip done and it made me giggle on the inside to think of her with a moustache.

After leaving the nail salon, Leela took me to a boring restaurant in midtown where they only served salads, but they did have more than a hundred different kinds. We looked at our menus and I put my napkin in my lap as Mum had taught me. Leela put her BlackBerry in her handbag and I felt a little alarmed because I never saw Leela without her BlackBerry close to hand before.

She swirled the ice in her iced coffee.

'Are you enjoying your little vacation in New York?' she asked.

'Yes,' I said.

'Good!' she replied. 'You must be so excited now about going back to Ireland?'

I didn't answer, busy poking at my salad, trying to identify some of the mysterious looking beans.

'Great!' she said, even though I hadn't said anything. 'And maybe, when you are grown up and have finished college, you will come back to New York for a visit. I'm sure Scott would like that.'

I shivered. The air conditioning was way too cold.

'Here,' she said. 'Have my scarf.'

'No thanks,' I said.

'How is your cookbook going?' I asked in an innocent voice.

Her eyes narrowed and she pursed her lips together.

'I haven't dated the right connections,' she answered, 'but I will get there.'

Then she smiled breezily.

'Isn't this fun?' she said, 'having a girls' lunch.'

I didn't answer.

She continued, 'I know how important it is to you to be in Ireland, back with all your friends and your godmother, Lainey is it?'

'Do you mean Janet?' I said.

'Yes, Janet, that's the one. I need you to give me her phone number and her email address.'

'What for?' I asked.

'So I can get the paperwork moving.'

'What paperwork?' I wondered.

'To transfer full custody of you to Janet.'

My jaw dropped.

'That's got nothing to do with you,' I told her.

'Oh, of course not, I'm just trying to save poor Scott some money by doing the paperwork myself instead of him having to pay another attorney to do it. That would be a terrible waste, especially when he is so strapped for cash and the clinic expenses are so high and he has that new receptionist's salary to worry about – Kelly.'

'Karen,' I corrected automatically.

'Do you want your uncle to have to pay thousands of dollars to a lawyer?' she said, in a fake shocked voice.

'No, of course not,' I said angrily. 'I just didn't realise anything had to be done, and won't Scott and I have to sign the papers?'

She shook her head.

'You are the child. You're not even allowed to read them.'

'It's my life,' I said angrily.

'But your life does not belong to you in the eyes of the law,' she said primly. 'Yes, Scott has to sign, but we can get them ready now. If I tell Scott before I do the work, he will want to pay my law firm's fees, which is what we are trying to avoid, isn't it?'

I poked again at the large, rubbery, yellowish beans in my salad.

'Here,' said Leela, pulling a little red notebook out of her bag and flicking it open and handing me a pen. 'Just write Janet's email address here, that will be enough.'

I hesitated.

'Oh! I'm so sorry, Evie,' she said gushingly.

'What?' I said.

'Are you afraid Janet doesn't want you anymore?'

'No, of course not!' I said hotly. 'Janet is one of the most loyal, best, greatest people I know. She would have me in a second, any time, no matter what.'

'So, there's no problem then,' said Leela crisply.

I pushed the pen and notebook back at her.

'I want to go home,' I said.

'Of course you do, sweetie, and you will be back in Ireland very soon. It must be lovely there, so beautiful with all those green fields and sweet little horses. I really must visit on my next trip to London.'

I didn't point out that I had meant Scott's apartment because I was sure Leela had known exactly what I'd meant.

'Whatever,' I said, and she tut-tutted at my rudeness, but stopped pushing to get Janet's email address.

I took the cross-town bus by myself back to Scott's apartment and I put the lunch with Leela completely out of my mind as if it never happened. I can do that sometimes.

Chapter 12

On Wednesday morning, Kylie called as Scott and I were finishing our breakfast bagels. I was ignoring Ben as punishment for chewing the tip of my elephant Ellie's trunk. As I chatted with Kylie, Ben gazed at me with sad, puppyish eyes, begging for cream cheese, and, I fondly imagined, forgiveness. Kylie was heading to Chelsea Piers with Greg Winters. It turns out that Kylie knows Greg. More than knows. They go to the same school and are good friends.

'Greg plays for the River Rats. That's a kids' ice-hockey team. They have a game today so I'm going to go watch and then I have my figure skating lesson. You guys could watch my lesson and we can all eat lunch afterwards.'

I hesitated. I had planned to help out Scott in the clinic.

'I'll ask Scott if he'll be okay this morning without me.'

Scott looked up from page six of the *New York Post*.

'I will do my very best to manage adequately without you,' he said solemnly. 'Don't stray from the Piers and I expect to see you back here no later than three. Have fun.'

'Thanks a million!' I replied.

The Rivers Rats' game was more exciting than I expected.

Greg was amazing. He swept up and down the ice so quickly and scored a goal against the New Jersey team.

'Woo-hoo!' yelled Kylie. 'Go Rats!'

'There were no fights,' Kylie said, a bit sadly, when the game ended.

Greg, still glowing from victory and from a fresh batch of angry-looking mosquito bites, sat on the bench beside me to watch Kylie's figure skating lesson. I was in awe. She was so graceful on the ice and she did some amazing spins.

'That's a double Axel,' Greg told me.

I thought she was fantastic, but her coach, a tall skinny woman in a blue and white tracksuit, yelled harshly at her several times. At the end of the lesson, I could tell the coach was having a go at Kylie although I couldn't hear what they were saying.

'Why is the bully coach being so mean to Kylie?' I asked Greg angrily.

Greg looked surprised.

'The coach is just trying to motivate her to do better, to be better. Kylie has a competition coming up.'

'It's not the Olympics,' I muttered.

'Not yet,' said Greg.

After Kylie had changed back into normal clothes, the three of us went for burgers and fries and shakes at the diner and had a great laugh. Kylie didn't mention her coach and she didn't seem upset at all.

'Your coach seemed a bit mean,' I ventured.

Kylie swung around so that her green-streaked ponytail

nearly landed in my raspberry-chocolate milkshake.

'Suzie is the best. She's the greatest coach in the Tri-state area. I'm lucky she is teaching me. She's tough on me because I haven't practised enough, and she's right.'

'Does Rachel come down on you to do better?' I wondered.

'Nooooo! My mom is so not the competitive type. She just wants me to be happy. I think she would prefer if I did not compete at all, if I just skated for fun, but I like competing. Sometimes I wish she was one of those pushy moms so I would be forced to practise more.'

I looked out the window as I drained the dregs of my milkshake. I spotted Finn, dressed in hockey gear, walking past the diner with a slim blonde girl. He saw us and waved with his hockey stick.

'Finn's too old and too good to play for the River Rats anymore. Now, he plays in a different league. He's their big star,' announced Greg proudly.

'Who's his girlfriend?' asked Kylie.

'Tamara something. She's a freshman at Nightingale-Bamford,' Greg said.

'That's one of the best private girls' schools in the city,' Kylie explained to me. 'A freshman is someone in their first year of high school.'

'She's very pretty,' I noticed.

'If you like blondes,' said Greg.

'She's too All-American, Gossip Girl slash cheerleader slash prom queen type. YAWN,' said Kylie.

The more I get to know Kylie, the more I like her.

There was a note waiting for me when I got home, written in green ink.

'Evie, the very old vacuum your uncle owns sucked up the trunk on your elephant yesterday. Sorry, Eurdes xx.'

I was horrified. I had punished Ben for nothing. I scrambled off to search for him straight away, but he was not in any of his normal places. Eventually, I found him lying under the receptionist's table in the waiting room of the clinic, gnawing on what looked suspiciously like a tube of Leela's lip-gloss. Good boy. I knelt down beside him. I knew he wouldn't understand the word 'sorry' but I wanted to say it anyway.

'I'm sorry, Ben.'

He licked my hand and he wagged his tail.

'Longest walk ever, coming up right now,' I told him and he happily stretched out his front paws so far that his belly hit the ground as I went off to search for his leash.

Later that evening, Ben and I hung around the clinic, keeping Snickers company. Snickers is a little, cotton-wool white bundle of tight curly fur, a Bichon Frise, which is a very popular breed of dog in Manhattan. He was staying overnight in the crate in the backroom of the clinic because Scott had to perform dental surgery on him the following morning. I was sitting cross-legged beside his crate, desperately yanking my almost bristleless hairbrush through an enormous knot when Scott walked in.

'What is it?' he asked, looking at my face screwed up in pain.

94

'The mother of all knots,' I answered.

Scott bent over to have a look, disappeared for a couple of minutes and returned with a scissors we use for trimming cat hair before operations and, with a decisive single snap, chopped off the large knot and handed it to me.

I stared at it, appalled.

'Scott, I can't believe you just did that.'

'What?' he said innocently. 'You have lots of hair. I have never seen a kid with so much hair; you won't even notice it's gone.'

I resolved to keep my hair issues away from Scott's trigger scissors hands in the future. Joanna would have been able to empathise but she was on a date with Stefan.

Joanna seems to like Stefan a lot because she is being pretty hush-hush about him and acting all girly. Although he's from Frankfurt he speaks English perfectly if a little stiffly, with a London accent. His hair is white-blonde and his eyelashes are so fair I thought he didn't have any when I first met him. He is huge, even taller than Scott, and has the largest feet I have ever seen. Stefan works for a hedge fund, which is some complicated finance job that has nothing to do with gardening. He doesn't seem like a bad guy. He's very polite. Last Tuesday, he took Mrs Rubenstein by the arm and helped her out of the waiting room, carrying Lulu in her cage, and hailed a taxi for them. Scott said he was just trying to impress Joanna. I'm not so sure. Stefan has nice manners. He's just boring. I don't think he can help it. He was probably born that way.

Scott and I have spied on him a couple of times, getting out of his Porsche to pick up Joanna from work.

Scott said, 'It's a crime against humanity to have a high-lighter-yellow Porsche.'

He had a point. The car was so not cool, but I think he might, totally understandably, feel a bit jealous of Stefan because Scott's Jeep is ancient and breaks down a lot, always at the worst possible times.

Maybe Scott secretly fancies Joanna without even realising it himself, but I could be totally wrong. When David and Mum first became friendly, I spent ages working on getting them together as a couple because I thought David fancied Mum like mad and I thought she fancied him too. When they eventually realised what I was up to, they sat me down for a *talk*.

David asked me, 'Evie, you know I'm gay, right, and you know what that means?'

'Yeeees,' I said, 'but I thought that might change, you know, on account of you falling in love with Mum.'

'I do love your mum very much as a friend but the being gay thing, that's not going to change.'

I felt very stupid because I was sure his being gay was just a detail, a little obstacle that could be overcome. I thought Mum was a bit lonely and could do with a nice, fun boyfriend like David and they both loved theatre so they had a lot in common.

As a result of the David – Mum romance fiasco, I completely lost confidence in my matchmaking instincts. I promised Mum I would cease all match-making activities. She said I was talented in other areas.

Chapter 13

After lunch yesterday, I skyped with Deirdre and Cate, my best friends in Dublin.

'It's been raining all day every day per usual,' claimed Cate gloomily.

Deirdre chipped in, bursting to give me all the news.

'Aoife McNally had a birthday party with a bouncy castle in her back garden. It was sad. She was mortified that her parents rented a bouncy castle as if she had turned nine instead of twelve. Fiona O'Hegarty's mum was wearing these super high black heels, the ones with the red soles – Christian Bootins.'

'You mean Christian Louboutins,' said Cate.

'Whatever! Stop interrupting me! I'm trying to tell Evie the story. Anyway, Mrs Hegarty must have had too much vino or something because she decided to have a go on the castle and one of her Lo … one of her shoes punctured it and the whole castle started to collapse. There were loads of little kids on it. They started screaming like mad and there was total chaos as all the parents tried to get to them. Poor Aoife was doubly mortified.'

'But she got some fantastic birthday pressies,' said Cate,

'like a turquoise mountain bike.'

'I hadn't finished,' said Deirdre. 'John Donaghy broke it off with Sarah and now he's going with Fauve Brennan. She's Mark O'Toole's cousin from Sandymount. She has a tattoo in Celtic script on her shoulder that says *Daughter of Ireland* or something like that, and she has peroxide streaks in her hair and her nose is pierced and she goes snowboarding in France every Christmas. She's supposed to be brilliant at it. Almost everyone from the class got invited to the church part of Miss Butler's wedding. Her dress was so gorgeous.'

'Sounds cool,' I said cheerfully.

'Will you listen to her? In America only what … seven weeks and already has an American accent,' said Deirdre.

'That's daft,' I said. 'No, I don't. No way, and I only managed to get two words in. How could you think I sounded American from that?'

'You have a bit of a twang,' said Cate.

'You'll probably lose it when you are back here a day,' she added reassuringly.

I didn't feel reassured.

'Tell us all about what's going on with you in New York,' said Deirdre. 'I'd kill to be there for a week.'

The phone call with the girls bugged me for the rest of the day. I asked Joanna about it later as I helped her disinfect the examining table.

'Do *you* think I sound American?' I wondered.

She laughed.

'No, definitely not.'

'Not even a tiny bit?' I persisted.

'No, you sound about as American as Kate Winslet.'

'Who?' I asked.

'The *Titanic* chick, the British one.'

'Oh.'

It was hard to feel reassured by someone who couldn't tell the difference between a British accent and an Irish one. I tried Scott next as we ate our take-out chicken burritos with extra guacamole.

'Do you think I've started to sound American?' I asked nonchalantly.

'Nah,' he said with his mouth full, 'you've picked up some American words and expressions but not the accent. Why?'

'It's just that some of the gang from Ireland were slagging me. They said I sound American. I don't want to go home with a new American accent.'

Scott wiped some of the guacamole carefully from his chin.

'Why do you care, Evie?' he asked briskly.

'I don't know. I guess I don't want to lose being me. I don't want to be the *American Evie*. That would just be weird. Where would *Irish Evie* go? I mean, where would *I* go?'

Scott offered me some of his tortilla chips as he thought about what I'd said.

I spoke up again.

'I'm not tough like Mum. She went through hundreds, maybe thousands, of auditions and dealt with so many rejections. One time, she got rejected five times in a single day. I don't want to be rejected for having an American accent, for being different.'

I felt a little panicky.

'It was hard enough fitting in when we settled back permanently in Dublin a couple of years ago.'

'Evie,' said Scott. 'What kind of accent you have is not important. It doesn't define you. You can be *you* no matter what your accent is like. Just be who you are. If that is different from others, so be it. When the Dublin kids realise that their teasing doesn't bother you, they'll get bored and move on to something else, like your blue hair.'

'My hair hasn't been blue in ages,' I said, 'but ok, I get your point.'

I mustn't have sounded completely convinced.

Scott sighed.

'Evie, you don't need a stamp saying *100% Irish* on your forehead, like a packet of Irish sausages. You are half-American and that's not so bad. We've got Thomas Jefferson and Bart Simpson and Marilyn Monroe and ice hockey and Harley-Davidson bikes and Quentin Tarantino and ... and ... and ... Brangelina and raspberry-chocolate milkshakes and JFK.'

'And RFK,' I said proudly, showing off a little.

'And Bobby,' he smiled.

'Who is Quentin Tarantino?' I asked.

'He's a movie director.'

'Can I watch one of his films?'

'No, you have to wait until you are older. Now, get out of here and take your multiple identities down to the clinic and see if Joanna needs any help.'

Chapter 14

I saw my first Broadway show last night. It was opening night for Mrs Winters' new musical, *Starchitect*. Greg invited Kylie and me. We had fantastic tickets, in the middle of the main section, three rows from the stage. Finn was also there with Tamara. She was wearing a shimmery, light gold, chiffon summer dress with flat, gold, gladiator sandals. With her golden hair swinging down her back, she looked like a gilded statue, surrounded by a halo of gold. She smiled at us and said my 'brogue' was 'cute'. I guess I didn't sound American to her.

'She's hurting my eyes,' said Kylie, putting on her pink cat eye sunglasses, not caring that sunglasses are not usually worn in theatres. I never saw Finn without his Rangers cap before. Kylie nudged me; the curtains were rising and she looked as excited with anticipation as I felt.

The musical was about three architects, two men and one woman, who enter a competition to build the new, highest building in the world in Shanghai, in China. They were not just work rivals; all three of them were in love with the same woman, a professional photographer named Lillian who had short, spiky, cranberry-red hair.

'Nobody would fall in love with that hair,' whispered Kylie.

During the play, the architects all cheat and do nasty things to each other to try to win the competition and to win Lillian. In the end, Lillian didn't choose any of them. However, none of them was really cut up about it because through the course of the show, each of them realised that what they actually loved most was the joy of designing a building. Nobody won the competition because the ruthless Chinese billionaire who had commissioned the building had a change of heart and decided to build good quality housing for the zillions of desperately poor Chinese factory workers instead of one big fancy office building. He and Lillian fall in love and walk off together into the smog at the end of the show, singing a duet.

We all squeezed through the crowds to reach backstage afterwards, Kylie coughing a little because the smog special effects were a little overpowering. It felt strange to be back in the theatre world again, strange and familiar at the same time. I kept expecting Mum to pop up and give me a sip of champagne out of her glass as she always did on opening night. But of course she did not.

Hordes of people crowded around Angela's chair. Angela is Finn's and Greg's mom. Although her hair is short and purple-ash grey, she looked beautiful. She wore a dark green, mid-length cape over a sherry coloured strapless dress. She didn't look anything like either Finn or Greg. When she saw us kids, she immediately sprang up from her chair, pushed her fawning admirers aside and came over and hugged Greg. She tried to hug Finn too, but he held back a little so she had to make do with rubbing his arm. She kissed Tamara and Kylie and me, twice each, which is very common in the theatre world and in Paris.

'Did you girls enjoy the show?' she asked.

'It was wonderful, really great,' gushed Tamara and Kylie in unison and Angela smiled.

'What about you, honey?' she asked me.

I nodded truthfully and she smiled, pleased.

'I saw your poor mother once, sweetheart … dear Alicia. She was on the stage in London. Six years ago or maybe it was seven. She was the most beautiful Rosalind.'

I was shocked to notice that tears came into her eyes. I mean – she saw my mum once in a play. She didn't know her at all, certainly not enough to cry for her. But I'm used to theatre people being overly dramatic. Tears rolling down her cheeks, Angela leaned down to envelop me in a hug and I felt dizzy and overpowered by the strong smell of her perfume, like incense at Easter mass, a smell that always makes me feel a little afraid. I stiffened. Finn pulled his mom gently away from me.

'*Vamos*! Let's eat, I'm starving,' he said.

'Yes, of course, darling,' Angela answered.

We walked a few blocks to a bistro, dodging around the clusters of tourists gawking at the billboards and the lights in Times Square.

'I will be on that billboard one day,' announced Kylie pointing to a giant electronic screen, displaying two actresses standing on a motorbike. Occasionally, Finn glanced behind to make sure Greg, Kylie and me did not get lost in the shuffle.

'He is so the older brother,' said Greg, in a resigned tone, slapping a mosquito on his neck.

The bistro had a long narrow bar, smoky mirrors and red leather banquettes around the sides. The *maitre d'* embraced Angela and led us to a large booth near the back. Other members of the cast and crew filed in from time to time and sat down at neighbouring booths.

We started with oysters, except for Greg, who has a shell-fish allergy, and Kylie, who hates them.

'I can't stand the slimy feel and the seawater taste,' she explained with a shudder.

Angela sat at the edge of the booth so she could nip out for cigarette breaks without everyone having to get up to let her out. She clearly enjoyed being the centre of attention. She was very funny and self-disparaging most of the time and I couldn't help liking her.

We didn't have to wait for the newspapers to come out in the morning with reviews of the show because the first show review appeared on a blog eleven minutes after the show ended. During the meal, more and more reviews went online and Daren, the director of the show, read them out in the restaurant and we cheered and clapped because they were all good except for one very sour one, which said that the actress who played the part of *Lillian* sounded like a raccoon in labour.

'There always has to be one hater,' said Finn, rolling his eyes, 'as if that guy knows what a raccoon in labour sounds like.'

Tamara laughed prettily and reached up and ran her hand quickly through his hair. I didn't like it.

Chapter 15

August has arrived and with it, the sticky heat that Frank had promised. Scott gave me the money to take Ben to the local grooming salon to get shaved down so he would be more comfortable in the humidity. Ben was prancing along as usual, stopping to sniff and to pee on the trunk of every tree on the sidewalk, especially on the tree trunks that other dogs had already peed on. But when we got to within a few metres of the grooming place, he stopped dead and would not budge, no matter how much I implored him. Eventually, I had to pick him up and carry him in, which caused me to sweat a ton so I looked like I had just stepped out of the shower. Once inside, he seemed resigned to his fate and went off pretty meekly with Meredith, the groomer.

When I picked him up a few hours later, he looked so different, much skinnier, like a shorn newborn black and white lamb, and he wore a bright yellow satin ribbon tied in a loopy bow around his neck. I knew Ben must hate that ribbon. He never wears clothes like so many of the dogs in Manhattan and the ribbon made him look like he was a girl. As soon as we were out of sight, I bent down and unwrapped him. He licked my hand, grateful to have a little dignity restored.

We got back in time to help Scott with the afternoon clinic. The first patient was Bailey, which is obviously a name for a small dog, a miniature poodle or a shih tzu. But, to my surprise, Bailey was a large, beautiful, eight-month old Doberman Pinscher with a friendly face.

Amanda is Bailey's 'Mommy'. She is about thirty years old. Her long, dark-brown hair was scraped tightly back from her face into a ponytail secured by a yellow elastic band. From the second we met, she talked in a hoarse, nasal voice, without pausing to breathe, about all the dogs she has ever had or known, which is a lot because she is a professional dog trainer and walker. She said she walks about fifteen dogs a day, five at a time. She also gives puppy training and obedience classes. I thought I recognised her. I remember seeing her in the Park with five dogs, all different sizes, on little leashes connected to a big leash. I noticed that she talked to them constantly, mainly about her difficult love life.

I helped Amanda lift Bailey up onto the examining table. She was still talking. She was sure that Bailey was going to be a champion in the show ring. I started to get the impression that when it came to dogs, Amanda was a bit of a know-it-all.

'Bailey's just got a bit of bleeding from his toe nails. I must have nicked one when I was cutting them yesterday, which isn't like me at all. I'm always so careful.'

Scott began to examine Bailey while Amanda regaled me with stories about the long line of Dobermans she had owned since she was a little girl, one of which had won 'Best in Breed' at the Westminster Dog Show in 1996.

'Wow!' I said, courteously, although I've never been overly impressed with dog show titles. Ben wouldn't be allowed to enter. Under dog show rules, you are not permitted to show neutered dogs and Ben was neutered when he was six months old because Scott thought that was the healthiest option for a dog living in New York City. And, the dog shows only allow one hundred percent pedigree dogs to take part and Ben is a half-breed. That is so snobbish and unfair. Many of the nicest and friendliest dogs that come into the clinic are mixed breeds, mainly adopted from shelters.

'We need to get some blood work done, just a few tests,' Scott told Amanda gently.

Amanda grimaced.

'Scottie,' she said loudly and he winced. 'I can't afford to pay for totally unnecessary tests. It's just a little nail problem. It was my fault. These things happen.'

Scott was firm.

'I think it is more serious than that. We need to do the blood tests. You can pay over time in small instalments.'

Amanda still looked doubtful but she acquiesced.

'Ok,' she mumbled and she kept up a stream of chatter to Bailey as Scott drew the blood.

I overheard Scott calling Amanda a few days later with the results. Bailey had von Willebrand disease, a blood disorder, which I gathered could be pretty serious. Scott told Amanda that it was similar to haemophilia in humans.

'It can't be cured, Amanda,' said Scott, 'but it can be managed. Bailey should be able to have a reasonably normal life. It's important that you avoid playing rough with him as even light injuries can cause problems.'

I couldn't hear Amanda's side of the conversation, but I felt sorry that her dreams of stardom at Westminster with Bailey had been shattered.

Not long after lunch, when I was cleaning out Sam's new tank, Janet telephoned to announce that she has a wonderful, new boyfriend, Brendan.

'He's a sound engineer,' she said, a little breathlessly. 'We met on the set of a new TV show filmed in Westport, a documentary about a family from Dublin who moved there to run a goat farm and open up a cheese and yoghurt shop. Remember – I told you all about it in my emails.'

'Oh yeah,' I said, privately thinking that the pilot had not sounded riveting.

'I have never been on a set with so many problems in my life,' she chattered. 'The director had a bad pint of Guinness or something because he ended up in hospital with a mysterious stomach ailment, and half the cheese turned out to be mouldy and we had to substitute fake cheese.'

She paused for breath.

'Anyway, about Brendan and me – we are thinking that I will move in with him, to his house in Bray.'

'That sounds a little fast,' I ventured.

But Janet wrongly jumped to the conclusion that I was thinking about myself.

'Love, there will be loads of space for you,' she emphasised. 'Brendan's house has four bedrooms and he has a back garden. He can't wait to meet you. He has heard all about you. It will be great craic the three of us living together. You are going to adore him. He's an expert at cooking spicy shrimp pad thai and he does brilliant, dead-on *Monty Python* impressions.'

'It was Mum that liked *Monty Python*, not me,' I said, absentmindedly, and then I immediately regretted sounding so bratty.

'He sounds really nice,' I added quickly.

That made her happy.

'He is,' she gushed. 'He doesn't have a hair on his head, but he's gorgeous. He's completely different to anyone I have ever gone out with before.'

'That can only be good,' I answered. 'I like him already.'

Janet giggled.

'Not long now, darling, you'll be back home in just under five weeks.'

Why didn't that make me feel excited? Maybe I was coming down with something, like heatstroke.

'Gotta run, miss you loads. Tell David I was asking for him and tell Brendan I look forward to meeting him, bye!' I said, and hung up.

Chapter 16

It has become our ritual to have break-fast on Friday mornings at Pier 72, a diner on the corner of West 72nd Street and West End Avenue. It's a real old-fash-ioned New York City diner with doughnuts under glass and egg-stained menus and an ancient, grumpy waitress, Velda, who barks at the customers and at the Ecuadorean busboys. They ignore her.

Scott always orders the same thing, two eggs over easy with an English muffin on the side. I alternate between pan-cakes and a Belgian waffle, which Scott refers to as 'syrup with a side of pancakes or waffles'.

'How can you eat that corn syrup?' he wondered.

'Very easily,' I responded, liberally drowning my pancakes.

He turned his attention to Joanna, who had joined us this morning. She also ordered what she always orders, Greek yoghurt with honey and fruit with a side of bacon and toast.

Joanna seemed distracted and fidgety.

'What's up?' Scott asked her.

'Do you know the charity group I volunteer with?' she asked.

113

'Yes, the children's literacy project – helping the kids in the projects in the Bronx learn to read.'

She nodded.

'I got railroaded into giving a talk to some of the high school kids next month about what my job is like – *What it Takes To Be A Vet*. I don't have a clue what to say. I would rather do fifty consecutive surgeries spaying cats, and with a cheap red wine hangover, than do this presentation.'

Scott grinned.

'Say that.'

'What?'

'There is your opening line. Just be yourself and be honest. Walk them through it.'

Joanna looked dubious.

Scott warmed to this theme.

'Tell them some of your funny stories about some of the incidents with the animals and the clients.'

'Like the time Herman, the white bulldog with the farting problem, kept doing nasty silent ones, and Eliot, the cute Asian guy who came in with Charley, his pet iguana, thought it was coming from you,' I interjected helpfully.

'You can talk about how, a lot of times, the patient we are really treating is the owner, not the pet,' added Scott. 'Tell them why you became a vet. Tell them that becoming a vet involves a lifetime of studying, hard work, late nights and lousy pay, but it's never dull and the patients make up for all the headaches.'

'Ok,' said Joanna. 'I'm starting to feel inspired.'

'Why don't you take Ben with you?' I suggested.

Joanna took off her glasses and cleaned them as she thought about that one.

'I could use Ben as a hypothetical patient, do a practical demonstration,' she said.

I felt a pang of guilt for volunteering Ben. He wasn't going to like this at all, but he had a tolerant nature. I resolved to make it up to him by putting some of Joanna's bacon in my napkin to treat him later.

'I could come with you for moral support,' Scott suggested.

Joanna waved him away.

'That's ok, Stefan already volunteered,' she said airily.

'The kids will really be able to relate to Stefan,' said Scott innocently.

'Maybe I should ask Leela instead – I'm sure taking time off work to interact with underprivileged kids would be right up her street,' replied Joanna, even more innocently.

'Why *did* you become a vet, Joanna?' I asked.

She smiled her wide, beautiful, Anne with an 'e' smile.

'You know the kid at school who is always finding and bringing home birds with broken wings to try to heal them, that kind of thing. Well, I was that kid. I always wanted to be a vet. I can't remember a time when I didn't want to be a vet.'

She began scribbling some notes of ideas for the presentation on the paper napkins.

'How long have I worked for you now, Scott?' she asked.

'Three years, four months, one week,' he answered immediately.

'And in all that time, I've never asked you what made you become a vet,' she said, with a question mark in her tone.

'You don't want to hear my boring becoming-a-vet story,' he said, draining the last of his orange juice.

'Yes, we do,' I replied.

He shrugged.

'Dr Lucas,' he said.

'Dr Lucas,' he repeated, more to himself than to us.

Joanna and I waited.

Scott sighed.

'I had a golden lab when I was a teenager. Try not to snigger openly, but her name was Goldie. She followed me everywhere. She was such a loyal dog and an incredible jumper. You should have seen how far she could jump from a pier into the water. She loved swimming; she was half dog, half dolphin. When I was sixteen, soon after I got my driving license, a group of us drove across the country to Montana on a camping trip. Just a bunch of privileged Connecticut kids goofing around in the wilderness. One night when we were pretending to be men, drinking beers around the campfire that took us about half a day to get started ...' and he laughed.

'Go on,' said Joanna.

'I realised Goldie was missing, so we divided into two groups and set off to find her. Poor Goldie, she had got her leg caught in a steel trap left by a poacher. When I found her, she was all matted with blood and, despite her tremendous pain, when I knelt beside her, she just gave a little whimper and licked my hand.'

He paused for a minute, remembering.

'We cut straight through that steel trap and I ran with her in my arms back to the car and set off looking for a vet. You have to remember this was late at night in the middle of nowhere. I stopped at the nearest gas station for directions. The woman there looked at me as if I was crazy to be out of my mind over just a dog. But she said, "Try old Lucas in the next town over," and she gave me directions.'

'I arrived at a dilapidated, clapboard cabin, all peeling paint with a rusted car in the front and heaps of junk all over the lawn. I ran up the steps to his porch and kept my finger on that bell until I heard someone yelling, "Alright, alright, no need to wake up the dead. I'm coming," and this old man opened the door.'

'He looked in bad shape, more like a homeless drug addict than a vet. He had a vest on that could have been white once, with gaping holes and some kind of dark pants held up by braces. His hair was long and grey and matted and he had a grey beard with bits of barbeque he had for dinner stuck in it. He smelt of stale beer and something else, maybe urine.'

'He took one look at Goldie and me and said, "Bring her in, son," and I followed him through into the back room where he saw the animals. I've never seen a poorer practice. He didn't have any modern equipment at all, just a few bits and pieces that looked like they had been around since the

117

Civil War and an ancient examining table, which had only three legs. "Put your leg there," he grunted. And I shoved my leg against the table to keep it up.'

'All night long, he worked on Goldie while I held up the table. He didn't say much. He just concentrated. When dawn finally came, he straightened up and he said, "We've done what we can, it's in God's hands now." I asked him about paying him, explaining I just had a credit card my parents had given me, and he laughed so hard that I thought his wobbly looking front teeth were going to fall out. "No credit cards here, son, what have you got in cash?" So I emptied my pockets and I had seven dollars and twenty-three cents. "That will do," he said and he put the money in his pocket and shuffled out of the room.'

'That's an incredible story,' said Joanna. 'So old Lucas cured Goldie and that inspired you to become a vet.'

Scott shook his head.

'No, Goldie died later that day, peacefully in my arms, and I buried her there in Montana. But I have never been able to forget the way Dr Lucas tried with what he had, which was little more than his own pair of hands. If it were not for him, I would probably have been a business major at college and right at this very moment I would be on a yacht, surrounded by a bevy of Victoria's Secret models.'

Joanna smiled and she put her hand on top of Scott's and I put my hand on top of hers.

'What have we got here, *The Three Musketeers*?' asked Velda, with a sniff, tearing out the bill and dropping it down on our table.

'Absolutely,' said Scott, winking at her, 'do you want to be d'Artagnan?'

'I've no time for your shenanigans, Dr Brooks, I have work to do,' and she shuffled off, but not before giving him a second free refill of coffee.

As we strolled back to the clinic, I asked Scott, 'did you get a new dog when Goldie died?'

'No' he said, 'I missed Goldie so much that I guess I was too much of a coward to get a new pet.'

'Until you got brave enough to get Ben,' I pointed out.

'Not exactly,' he said.

'I got Ben in a poker game. Texas hold 'em.'

'Oh my God. You won Ben in a card game. That is sooo cool,' I said.

'Who said anything about winning? The *loser* had to take Ben.'

'What?'

'Ben was the youngest puppy in a litter of nine born to Sidney's sister's English cocker spaniel. They found good homes for all the puppies. But Ben's new owners brought him back, claiming he was untrainable. Now, who could think that?'

Joanna started laughing and Scott did his pretending-to-be-offended face.

'I still maintain that Sidney and her sister put something in my beers during that poker game,' he moaned.

It was a very interesting morning.

Chapter 17

I called Kylie this morning to see if she wanted to come with me to my horse-riding lesson and meet Luna, the horse I always ride. My riding instructor assigned Luna to me because she is an Irish draught horse, which she thought would suit me. Kylie said she couldn't make it.

'Why not?' I asked.

'Because I have the adopted kids' club today.'

'Can orphans join as well?' I asked.

'No, I don't think so. I think you have to be adopted.'

That didn't feel fair.

'Maybe I will text Greg to see if he can go,' I said, thinking out loud.

'Duh, no he can't,' said Kylie. 'He'll be with me.'

'But you just told me that only adopted kids can go,' I said huffily, wondering if she had invited Greg but not me.

'Greg *is* adopted. Didn't you know that?'

'What?' I said. 'But I've met his parents.'

'You met his *adoptive* parents,' said Kylie. 'Finn and Greg are from Wisconsin. Their dad abandoned them when Greg was a toddler. I think their mom was into alcohol or drugs, or both, and she couldn't cope, so she gave them up for adoption. They were in a few foster homes. Greg doesn't remember much. He was only four and a half when the Winters adopted them.'

I felt stunned.

'They never said anything,' I protested.

'Do you go around announcing to people that you are an orphan?' Kylie asked.

'No, you know I don't. Of course not.'

'So adopted people don't go around saying, "Hey, guess what? I'm adopted."'

'Okay, okay, I get it,' I said. 'Have fun today.'

'You too. Enjoy the horseback riding and don't fall off.'

'I won't,' I promised, wondering why Americans say 'horse*back*' riding. Where else on a horse could you ride?

I very nearly did fall off when I was doing a posting trot around the indoor arena.

'Concentrate, Evangeline,' called out Danielle. 'You are in dreamland. Luna is in charge of you and it should be the other way around.'

'Sorry,' I said.

Danielle was right. I had been thinking about how Finn's and Greg's dad had abandoned them, just like my dad abandoned me and he hadn't even met me. But I could never, ever, in a million years imagine my mother giving up on me. She would never have done that. I felt bad for Greg and Finn. I was still thinking about them when Scott drove us home.

'You're very quiet today, Evie,' he said, questioningly.

121

'What's on your mind?'

'I feel sorry for Finn and Greg because their mother gave them up for adoption,' I answered simply.

'Don't feel sorry for them; they wouldn't like it and they are fine. More than fine. They have parents who love them and they have each other. Find another cause.'

Scott was right. The Wisconsin Winters did not need or want my pity.

'I did my first jump today,' I told Scott. 'At least, I think it could be classified as a jump – the pole was so close to the ground that the jump was over before I could blink.'

'Starting small is good,' said Scott. 'We should order you some riding breeches online. They'll be more comfortable for you to ride in.'

'No thanks,' I said. 'My jeans are fine and I'm only going to be here a few more weeks anyway.'

'So you still plan on going back to Ireland?' said Scott.

I nodded, waiting for him to say something more, but he just turned on the radio and began singing along.

'Who's that?' I asked.

'That is the late, great Johnny Cash.'

'Who's he?' I asked.

'Who's he?' Scott stuttered. 'We have a lot of work to do on your musical education.'

That evening, Scott dropped me off at Kylie's place to hang out. It wasn't nearly as much fun as usual because of another visitor; a thirteen-year old named Camille. When I first saw her, I thought she looked exquisitely pretty and sophisticated with her white-blonde hair tied up in intricate double Dutch braids.

'Did your mom do your hair?' I asked.

She laughed in a contemptuous way.

'As if! I got it done yesterday in the braid bar at the salon on the ninth floor in Bergdorf Goodman. You really should try it.'

I had never heard of Bergdorf Goodman.

'It's a high end department store on Fifth Avenue,' explained Kylie, seeing my mystified look.

Camille looked at me as if only someone who had lived her entire life on the moon would not know Bergdorf Goodman. A couple of hours later, I was wondering how I could possibly have thought Camille was pretty. She has tiny squinty eyes and a mean mouth.

When Camille went to the bathroom, Kylie gave me the lowdown on her. Her mom is American and her dad is French. Her parents are mega rich. Her father works at the same French investment bank as Tamara's father. Tamara is her cousin.

'Camille used to go to school at the Lycée Français de New York, but she is transferring to my school this year,' said Kylie, grimacing.

Soon after Camille came back from the bathroom, Rachel came into Kylie's bedroom with a tray of glasses of home-made lemonade and stopped to chitchat for a while. Camille kept showing off by speaking in French whenever Kylie or Rachel asked her something and then doing this annoying little shake of her head and saying, 'Oh, sorry, I keep forgetting, you can't speak French'. After about the third time she did this, I interrupted her rudely ... in French, which gave her a very satisfying shock.

I learned French when Mum and I lived in Paris. Mum was dead proud. I didn't have a word of French when we arrived, but after a few weeks, I realised that I could often understand what people were saying. By the time Mum's play ended, I was gabbing away as if I had lived in France my whole life. When we moved to Dublin, Mum gave acting classes to Delphine, an au pair from Marseilles who worked for a family in Foxrock. In exchange, Delphine dropped around to our flat and chatted to me in French for an hour or so every week.

Camille said, 'Oh, you speak French,' in a disinterested voice and didn't ask me any questions about it. But she quit speaking in French. Kylie and I exchanged glances. I could tell she was thrilled that I was able to take Camille down a peg or two. I don't think I have met anyone as full of herself since Amy McCann, even including Leela.

By the time Camille's mom came to pick her up, we were heartily fed up with her. Camille's mom was so thin with such a large head that she looked like an illustration from a Roald Dahl book. It was sickening the way Rachel sucked up to her. To be honest, I lost some of my respect for Rachel and I couldn't quite make eye contact with her. I excused myself and slipped back into Kylie's bedroom.

Kylie followed me a few minutes later.

'Mom does it for me,' she said quietly.

I felt embarrassed that Kylie read my thoughts.

'She needs Camille's mom to buy paintings from the gallery so she can pay for my ice-skating lessons and my school fees and violin camp.'

I felt like I was buried up to my neck in an entire dirty garbage load of shame. I knew exactly what Kylie was talking about. I tried to explain it to her.

'One time, when I was about seven, we were living in London and flat broke, Mum took a crappy job in which she had to dress up in a rooster costume and hang out on Tottenham Court Road, handing out leaflets for a fast food chicken burger chain. One cold, rainy afternoon, a crazy old man with some morbid hatred of chickens walked up to her and spat on her. Mum cried that night, and she hardly ever cried. Well, at least, she hardly ever let me see her cry. She said it was so disgusting and humiliating to be spat on that she wished the guy had beaten her up instead.'

Kylie and I tried to decide which was worse, being beaten up or spat on. We decided it would depend on how badly you got beaten up. We could very easily make up our minds about a choice between freezing to death and being burnt alive. Kylie chose death by fire. I thought that was totally mad. There is nothing I am more afraid of than being roasted alive, so I didn't even need a second to think about it.

'But anyway,' I said to Kylie, 'the point is that Mum got up the next day and put that stupid costume back on and went back out there because she needed the money to pay

for rent and food and clothes for me and all that. If she didn't
have me, she could have just gone to stay with a friend or
something.'

'Does it make you sad to talk about your mom?' Kylie
asked.

'No. Yes. I don't know. Sometimes yes, sometimes no.'

'I wish I could have met her,' Kylie said.

I smiled.

'I'm sure she would have loved you. She liked people with
what she called flair.'

I told Kylie I wanted to be a good friend and share the
Camille burden this summer. She responded by enveloping
me in a massive hug. There was never much hugging with
my friends in Ireland. I don't know why. It's just not something we did. When we were very little kids, four and five
years old, we used to hold hands when we went on school
excursions, but that was it. All this hugging Americans do
seemed really weird at first. But I'm getting used to it. I think
I kind of like it.

Chapter 18

I am upset. 'Upset' doesn't really cut it. I'm angry and super, super upset. I hate that slithering, sneaky, pig-ugly, thinks-she's-a-princess Leela. What am I thinking, calling her a pig? Arnold, the potbellied pig, is a thousand times better looking than Leela. But let me back up, all the way to this morning. Indirectly, it was kind of Scott's fault. He has this very irritating rule that I'm only allowed to use his iPad for an hour every day and I had already used up my hour by noon. That was a major problem because I have almost reached expert level on a new game app, which features a teenage, aboriginal girl who kills drug pushers and other bad guys with a boomerang while roaming the Australian outback. I just seem to have an enviable knack with a cyber boomerang.

Scott and Jake had decided on the spur of the moment to play squash. They had booked the court for only an hour and they were in such a rush that Scott dashed out without his phone. It seemed a perfect opportunity for some necessary extra iPad time, but I decided to take precautions in case he came home early. To avoid possible detection, I hid with the iPad behind the black sofa in the living room. It was quite comfortable on the floor there with my legs stretched out. I had some cushions and a bar of real Cadbury's chocolate, my favourite, a golden crisp that Janet had sent to me in the post. I muted the sound on the iPad and was concentrating hard when I heard the key turn in the door and the impatient click-clacking sound of high heels on the wooden floorboards.

Peering under the sofa, I glimpsed Leela's purple patent slingbacks. She called out in an antsy, peevish tone, 'Scott, are you here?'

Silence.

'Evangeline? Anyone?'

I briefly thought about answering but rejected the idea. I could get stuck with Leela for half an hour or more. Maybe she would just leave. No such luck. As Leela sat down, the sofa sagged in the middle, squeezing my knees painfully so that I nearly yelped. I heard her punching out a number on her BlackBerry.

She began speaking to her friend, Kirsten, about her usual woes, the pain-in-the-ass clients, the colleague who had bad-mouthed her to the senior partner, the mustard stain on her white blazer that the incompetent dry cleaners had failed to get out. I blocked her out, focusing on my boomerang until the sound of my own name caused me to lift my head.

'Scott is driving himself into bankruptcy over Evie. First it was horseback riding lessons. That was just the beginning. Now, he is talking about private school.'

Pause.

'He will probably want to provide her with her own car and driver next,' she snapped.

I couldn't hear Kirsten's response.

'Yes, she is supposed to go back to Britain, or Ireland, or wherever, in September, but Scott has given her the choice. I tried to get the contact details for the mother's friend in Ireland from her but she blanked me out. I am TERRI-FIED that she is going to stay here. You know, if freckled little orphan Annie hadn't popped up, Scott and I would definitely be engaged by now.'

'We never do fun things anymore,' Leela complained. 'I can't remember the last time we ate at a half-way decent res-taurant. We never went to the Hamptons once this summer. Scott always feels he has to be with that weird kid.'

Oh, I'm the weird one, I thought bitterly.

Leela continued to rant.

'It's all that bohemian, college drop-out, hippy-dippy, scattered sister's fault, dying and dumping her kid on Scott like that. You will not believe this but, apparently, she didn't even have a life insurance policy. Scott was her life insurance policy.'

For a few seconds, I just heard her say, 'Mm, ok, mm'.

Then, she started up again.

'The stupid, stinky dog and the constant stream of germ-ridden animals was bad enough, but now a kid as well, and soon she's going to turn into a moody teenager. It's intolera-ble! Can you imagine having a teenage waif hanging around all the time, staring at me with that freaky stare she has?'

My mouth dropped open. I don't have a 'freaky stare'. I heard a mumbled voice from the other end of the phone.

Leela broke in, 'I can't believe I ended up in a relationship with a practically penniless vet, while someone like Joanna Barrett, who can barely walk in flat shoes without falling, lands a wealthy hedge fund guy. It doesn't make sense.'

Again, there was a pause.

'Yes,' Leela conceded, 'Scott is super hot. And, if he listened to me, with those looks, his charm, and his people skills, he could have it totally made. You remember that guy Donald, the one I represented in defending the paternity and child support case? The mother was so desperate I was able to settle it for almost nothing. Anyway, Donald is a producer at a new local cable channel and he is putting together a TV show about a veterinary surgeon based in Manhattan. Carefully selected hotties will bring in their pets to the studio for his advice. It's bound to be a hit. You can barely walk half a block in this city without tripping over ten little hairy puffballs. Manhattan is teeming with animal lovers. And if the show is a hit, which it will be, then it will be syndicated nationally. Ker-ching.'

More silence.

My breathing seemed so loud. I clamped my hand over my mouth, but that seemed to make it worse as I struggled for air between my fingers.

But Leela didn't notice.

'Of course, I have suggested to Scott that he should audition for the show,' she wailed. 'I have been trying to get him interested for a month now, but he just won't bite. It is sooooo frustrating.'

More mumbling.

'Yes,' said Leela, thoughtfully, 'Scott does have a keen appreciation for the finer things in life. I think his reluctance is really because of the little leprechaun. I have to make sure she definitely returns to Leprechaun Land in September. Then, I am certain I could persuade Scott to do the show and we will be engaged by New Year's Eve, maybe even *on* New Year's Eve, which would be a nice touch. I want to have the wedding next May, it's such a chic month to get married.'

I don't know what Kirsten said in reply, but Leela cackled and said, 'I'm hardly the wicked stepmom. The kid will be better off back there. She doesn't belong here. She doesn't belong with Scott. I'm really doing Scott a favour. He'll be secretly relieved when his financial headache is gone and his conscience will be clear and he won't have to work thousands of hours in the basement anymore.'

Oh no, I thought as I heard the familiar, soft, flip-flop patter of Ben's snowshoe-like paws as he entered the living room. He paused right beside Leela and I saw his head duck down under the sofa. His large brown eyes met mine and he sniffed.

'Oh no, please!' I whispered. 'Please Ben, not now, don't give me away.'

I felt frantic. Ben doesn't even understand the command 'sit'. He's never going to get this.

But, to my astonishment, he didn't start barking. His head

withdrew from under the sofa. A couple of minutes later, as Leela talked about her prospective bridesmaids, I got a waft of noxious, rotten egg fumes mixed with kitty litter smell. Ben had let loose one of his silent, most deadly brand of farts – The Mother of All Farts. The smell reached Leela's nostrils a few seconds later.

'Ewwww!' I heard her exclaim. 'It's that gross, disgusting dog again. I have to get out of here. I have an appearance in Family Court downtown this afternoon. Talk later, sweetie.'

A few seconds later, the door slammed. I let out my breath in one big gasp and crawled out into the open, iPad forgotten. First things first – an enormous hug and some Scooby treats for Ben. Then, I had to think. I felt like throwing up. I felt like punching Leela in her silly face. No, I felt like decapitating her with a boomerang.

Chapter 19

I sat on the bottom branch of the per-
fect hanging-out tree, between Kylie and Greg. Kylie deli-
cately licked an Emack & Bolio's Swiss chocolate and mint
ice-cream cone. Greg obsessively scratched a swollen mosquito bite on his left ankle. I had already told them the gist
of Leela's evil scheme to turn Scott into a puppet vet on TV
and then marry him, but I left out everything she had said
about Mum and me.

'Leela de Vil MUST be stopped!' Kylie announced melodramatically.

'How do you always manage to eat ice cream without it
dripping?' Greg asked. 'It's like an exception to some laws of
physics or something.'

'Could we please focus?' I said impatiently. 'Hang on!
How *do* you manage to eat ice cream without it dripping?'

'I was born this way,' said Kylie complacently.

'Ok. Back to Leela. I can't believe Scott cares enough about
her to get tangled in her nasty little web. His practice means
everything to him. He's not going to abandon it and Joanna
to go play at being the hot version of Cesar Millan on TV.'

'I think Cesar Millan is cute,' said Kylie.

I sighed in frustration.

Kylie finished her waffle cone without any crumbs or broken pieces falling on her. Straightening imaginary creases from the skirt of her floral print sundress, she said, in a wise sounding voice, 'Scott's a guy so he's capable of doing very dumb things.'

'Sorry. Nothing personal, Greg,' she added.

'And before you know it, Scott and Leela are married with a baby on the way,' she continued darkly.

'The thought of a mini-Leela is too horrible to consider,' I said.

'The baby would have Scott's genes too,' Greg pointed out reasonably, transferring his attention to the mosquito bites on his arms.

'Is this what you guys meant when you talked about helping me?' I asked, 'because I'm not finding it super duper helpful.'

Greg laughed and Kylie put her arm around me.

'Like I said, Leela has to be stopped.'

'Yes,' I conceded. 'But how? We need a plan.'

'Why don't you just tell Dr Brooks everything you heard Leela say?' asked Greg.

Kylie immediately shook her head.

'Leela's a divorce attorney so she is an expert at twisting the facts. She'll say how terrible she feels that Evie misunderstood her, yada yada. *And* she is the grownup. Scott will believe her and Evie is the one that will look bad for hiding behind the couch.'

'I wasn't exactly *hiding* behind the sofa!' I exclaimed, indignantly. 'I was minding my own business. Leela had no business being there. She doesn't even live there.'

'What about talking to Dr Barrett?' asked Greg.

'I'd like to tell Joanna,' I admitted, 'but that would mean putting her in the middle between Leela and Scott, and that doesn't feel right.'

We sat without speaking for a few minutes, listening to the sounds of the Little League players drifting on the breeze from the Great Lawn. A tall man wearing a camel overcoat despite the intense heat walked past us and then stopped and turned around.

'Do you kids know where Strawberry Fields is? I think I've been walking around in circles.'

Another John Lennon fan. Kylie jumped up and gave him careful, precise directions.

'By the way, there are no strawberry bushes there,' she added, 'just so you are not disappointed.'

He thanked her and went on his way.

'We need a plan!' I repeated.

'A play,' said Greg.

I stared at him.

'Yes,' I said slowly, 'a plot, a cast of characters and a theme.'

'Let's go to my mom's place to brainstorm,' said Greg. 'She has this play script software we can use. It's fantastic! If you get stuck when you're writing, you just hit a prompt key and it comes up with all kinds of possible turns the plot could take.'

I felt excited and the beginnings of something suspiciously like *hope*.

'Sidney,' I said, triumphantly.

'Who is Sidney?' asked Greg.

'She's Jake's wife. She produces special effects for films. They live in Brooklyn and they have a very cute baby, Katie, who looks Korean, like Sidney. We went to brunch with them last Sunday and it was so obvious that Sidney and Leela hate each other and I heard Sidney tell Joanna that Scott only goes out with Leela because he is scared of love.'

'That's romantic,' sighed Kylie.

'I don't get girls sometimes,' said Greg. 'That doesn't sound romantic at all.'

'The point is,' I said, 'I'm sure Sidney would be thrilled to help me rescue Scott.'

'Help *us*,' said Kylie and Greg together.

I was touched.

'Thanks, guys.'

Chapter 20

The heat was intense in the city this evening, but I was utterly fed-up of being stuck inside in the air conditioning. I wandered over to the Park, hoping for a breeze. Ben put his head out the door with me but, recoiling from the heat, he sensibly changed his mind and returned indoors. Set among the small plot of pine trees north of the Delacorte Theatre are two sets of swings, one for toddlers and the other for bigger kids. I sat on a swing, tucked my skirt between my knees and pushed off. Higher and higher, I climbed. I leaned back into the air, my hair sweeping against the dusty, sandy ground.

'Hi, Evie,' said a familiar voice.

I instantly stuck out my feet to slow myself down and bring the swing to a stop.

Finn leaned his hockey stick up against the pole and sat on the swing next to mine. I wondered desperately if, despite the tucked-in skirt, my knickers had been showing. If they were plain white, it would not be a complete crisis, but I had a horrible feeling that they were the pair with the teddy bears holding birthday candles.

There was no possible way I could have a quick peep to check.

A hardback library book stuck out of Finn's backpack.

'What's it about?' I asked, indicating the book and trying to forget about my knickers.

'It's the biography of a professional ice-hockey player from Vancouver.'

'Good?' I asked.

'Nope, the dude is a little smug.'

Into my mind floated questions I wanted to ask Finn, but I never seemed to have the right opportunity. I plunged in.

'I was wondering if you were mad when you ran away… and when that person called the police?'

'Nooooo …' he said slowly. 'I wasn't mad.'

I felt astounded.

'But he turned you in and ruined everything. Maybe you would still be in Wisconsin if that nosey guy had minded his own business.'

Finn picked up his hockey stick and fiddled with it.

Without looking at me, he said, 'Evie, I was "the nosey guy", as you call it.'

'What?' I said, 'I don't get it.'

'I was the nosey guy,' he repeated. 'I was the anonymous caller who tipped off the police. I told them there was an underage kid working at the gas station who looked like a runaway and they should check it out.'

'But why?' I asked, puzzled.

'Because I wanted to be found. I wanted to come back to New York. I hadn't planned on running away forever. I picked Wisconsin because I kept in touch with one of my foster brothers who I thought might be able to help us. Also, I figured since we came from there, it would be the first place they'd look. But adults can be so dumb sometimes. They kept the search for us focused on the tri-state area.'

I couldn't think of anything to say.

Finn continued, 'It wasn't my dream to spend my life pumping gas and eating ninety-nine cents tacos. I just wanted to try to shake up our parents, to make them realise that they were being played by the lawyers, that they should dump the whole stupid divorce litigation.'

'And it worked,' I said.

'Yeah, eventually.'

'Look around you, Evie,' he said, waving in the direction of the Time Warner Building to the south.

'This is *NEW YORK CITY!*' he said in a radio presenter's voice.

Then he switched back to his normal voice. 'I would rather be a panhandler on the streets in New York than a king any-where else. Well, unless I was on a professional hockey team. For that, I would go anywhere.'

I thought about what he said, idly tracing in the dusty sand with my left foot.

'There's a small fishing town, not much more than a vil-lage,' I said, a little shyly, 'where my godmother Janet's parents live. It's called *An Daingean*, that's "Dingle" in English, and it's right on the most western tip of Ireland and it's the most beautiful place on the planet. I spent most of my summers there. You can stand on the cliffs jutting out over the Atlantic and feel the spray from the waves crashing against the cliffs and you can feel the wind. The wind is different there and it doesn't matter whether you are a panhandler or a king or a queen or a sports star, you can just be.'

'Profound,' said Finn. 'You think a lot,' and then he added teasingly, 'I bet they don't have an ice-hockey team, *The Dingle Icebreakers!*'

'No ice hockey,' I admitted.

Suddenly, he jumped off his swing so swiftly that it flew into the air with a clanking sound. He stood directly in front of me, his fists clenched. I couldn't understand his sudden anger.

'I haven't told anyone that I ratted myself out', he said fiercely, looking me straight in the eye. You'd better not tell anyone, not Greg, not Dr Brooks, nobody.'

'No, of course I won't,' I said indignantly. 'Don't get your knickers in a twist.'

'What? Oh, knickers are underwear right?'

I nodded.

'Ok,' he said, visibly relaxing. 'I don't know why I even told you about the call.'

'I don't know why you told me either,' I said honestly and he laughed.

'Come on, Irish fishing village girl,' he said, not in a mean way. 'I'll walk you home; I'm heading that way.'

Chapter 21

Chaos reigned in the clinic on Saturday morning. First, Karen called in sick, claiming she needed to go to the dentist due to severe pain in her wisdom teeth. Scott was sceptical. Karen had thrown a big, basketball-themed thirtieth birthday party the evening before for Jerry, her firefighter boyfriend from Staten Island. Scott had been on call, but Joanna had gone along.

'How was the party?' I asked her curiously.

Joanna shrugged in a non-committal way.

I persisted.

'But what was it like? What does a basketball theme really mean? What kind of food did Karen have?'

Joanna took off her glasses and rubbed her tired eyes.

'Buckets of chicken wings with blue cheese dip. Nearly everyone wore Knicks jerseys, and Knicks games played constantly on two enormous flat screen televisions and there were balloons and a blow-up, life-sized Jeremy Lin doll.'

'He's a player,' she added.

I nodded.

'I know. Greg and Kylie love him.'

Joanna groaned, 'I haven't seen so many kegs of beer since

I was in college.'

She began to grind some white medical powder viciously with a pestle and mortar.

'Did Stefan enjoy the party?' I wondered.

The pestle stilled.

'Funny you should ask that. No, he didn't. He wanted to leave after about fifteen minutes.'

'Why?' I asked.

'Because he didn't want to get his hands dirty mixing with the rednecks,' volunteered Scott, who had apparently been listening in.

Joanna's face flushed an angry red colour, a shade darker than her hair. She opened her mouth to speak, but then shut it again, satisfied herself with throwing Scott a dirty look, and began to grind the cat medicine even more aggressively, as if Scott's head was in the bowl.

Scott didn't apologise. He very rarely does. He ran his hand quickly through his hair.

'Evie, will you step up to the plate and be our receptionist today?'

I'm starting to understand the baseball metaphors they use here all the time.

'Sure,' I responded and headed out to the reception desk.

Four hours later, the backlog of dogs, cats, two guinea pigs, a ferret and a cockatoo had passed in to the examining room and out again. Just as I was considering a lunch run, the door opened and in stepped a woman, about forty-five years old, with dyed cotton candy pink hair, carrying a tiny monkey dressed in a red and white gingham dress and wearing a doll-sized, peroxide blonde wig.

The woman did not seem perturbed to find a child behind the desk. I liked her for that straight away.

'Hi. I am Lorraine Horrocks and this is my monkey, Marilyn. She has completely gone off her food, the poor little angel. She just sits around the apartment, making little moaning sounds.'

On cue, Marilyn emitted a pitiful moaning sound. I reached out and stroked her tiny, soft, furry head.

'You can go right through. Dr Brooks will see her straight away.'

'Thank you,' she said and she put Marilyn on the floor. Marilyn had a pink leash attached to a crystal-encrusted collar. Lorraine tugged on the leash and Marilyn scampered after her through the doors. I quickly placed a bell on the counter with a note saying, 'Please ring for attention' and followed Marilyn. I couldn't miss this.

Scott was weighing Marilyn when I walked in.

'Three pounds,' he announced and took the opportunity to give me a brief lesson.

'Marilyn is a capuchin monkey. They come from South America. They typically live in groups of between ten to thirty and spend most of their days hanging out, surfing trees and looking for food. They are highly intelligent.'

'I got Marilyn a toy piano and I'm teaching her to play "Happy Birthday",' interjected Lorraine proudly, gazing fondly at Marilyn as if she were her little girl.

Scott glanced at me. I knew what he was thinking. He is vehemently opposed to humans owning wild animals as pets and treating them like children. But he smiled at Lorraine in a compassionate way and I could tell he wasn't about to give her a lecture.

'What are you feeding her?' he asked.

'Jars of baby food,' replied Lorraine, 'but she hasn't touched a bite in twenty-four hours.'

'Is she going to be alright?' she asked, anxiously.

'Let's take a look at her,' said Scott, carrying Marilyn from the scales to the examining table. Marilyn put her tiny left hand around his neck. I leaned in to get a better look and she reached out and grasped my little finger and looked up at me with her little brown pinkish eyes.

'Conjunctivitis,' announced Scott.

'Oh, that doesn't sound so bad,' said Lorraine.

'I think it might be a sign of a more serious underlying problem,' answered Scott gently. 'I think she might have measles.'

'But she's been vaccinated against measles,' protested Lorraine.

'Unfortunately, vaccination does not always work,' replied Scott.

The bell from the waiting room rang so I peeled Marilyn's tiny fingers away and ran to see who was waiting.

I was surprised to find Tamara, Finn's girlfriend, carrying an adorable golden puppy in her arms. Finn stood behind her.

144

'Hi Evie,' she said and she smiled her beautiful smile at me.

I would love to say that it was a fake smile, but that would be untrue. Her blonde hair was tied in a fishtail braid. She wore high-waisted, neon blue shorts with a frilly, white, cami top. Blue eyeliner made her eyes seem even bluer and she wore pink lipstick that perfectly matched the mini handbag swinging off her shoulder. I don't wear makeup yet. Mum said that I should wait until I am fourteen. I felt grubby and dull and babyish.

'How's Sam?' asked Finn and it felt like we had never had that encounter on the swings.

'Sam's doing great,' I said. 'His leg is healing perfectly and it should be good as new by the end of the summer.'

'This is Patrick,' said Tamara, 'a Goldendoodle puppy that Finn got me from an animal shelter for my birthday.'

'The people at the shelter think that he is about seven months old,' said Finn.

'What kind of dog is a Goldendoodle?' I asked.

'A mix between a poodle and a golden retriever,' answered Tamara. 'Isn't he the sweetest, cutest puppy you have ever seen?'

I looked at his tiny, pale gold curls and his sweet face.

'Yes,' I replied, although I know from photographs that Ben was even cuter than that as a puppy.

'What kind of symptoms is he experiencing?' I asked, adopting a professional tone.

'Oh, none, he seems very healthy, but the shelter people recommended that we take him to get a check-up by a local vet and Finn told me your uncle is a great vet, worth the trip over to the west side.'

'Right now he's looking at a monkey that might have measles', I said, 'but if you guys want to sit down, he should be finished very soon.'

Tamara flashed her beautiful white teeth again and sat down.

Finn lingered by the desk.

'Greg told me you're going back to Ireland next month.'

I nodded. I hoped that maybe he would say something nice like he would miss me, but he didn't.

Marilyn came scampering through the door with her leash trailing behind her and began to run in circles around the table with the magazines, occasionally making detours to send cans of dog food flying off the nearby shelves.

'That monkey doesn't seem too sick,' said Finn, and he scooped her up as she passed by on her fourth lap and handed her to Lorraine, who was uselessly chasing her around the table and panting for breath.

'The little monkey is so sweet,' said Tamara.

'In that Marilyn Monroe get-up, she seems more like the Bride of Chucky than sweet,' Finn said to me in a low voice, so Lorraine would not hear him.

'Dr Brooks can see Patrick now,' I said.

Tamara stood up.

'That's Ben, your dog, right?' she said pointing at Ben who had been unhappily disturbed from his all-morning nap by Marilyn's antics.

'Yes, well he's my uncle's dog.'

'We should organise a doggie play date for him and Patrick,' she suggested.

'Thanks, but Ben's not a big fan of other dogs. I mean, he will acknowledge them by sniffing their butts but he never seems to be all that interested in them. Sometimes, we call him Pinocchio.'

'Why?' she asked.

'Because he thinks he is a human boy, not a dog. We don't know how to break the news to him. We showed him his reflection in the mirror but he just does his "I'm scared" bark at it. He doesn't realise he's barking at himself.'

Finn picked up Patrick with one hand and guided Tamara by placing his other hand on her back.

'See you later, Evie and Pinocchio,' he said.

Chapter 22

'Our plot has more holes in it than Swiss cheese,' I observed glumly, flicking through the newly printed pages of the script we had laboured over for more than a week.

'It will never work,' said Kylie.

'Pessimists,' said Greg, trailing a carrot piece in front of Dr Pepper.

I looked around the room curiously. At his dad's Park Avenue apartment, Greg had his own room but on 'B' weeks, he had to share a room with Finn at his mom's place.

'You spend 'A' weeks with your dad and then every second week is a 'B' week and you live here with your mom?' asked Kylie.

'Basically, yes,' said Greg, 'but it's a little more complicated than that; sometimes Mom and Dad switch weeks or chop them up. And it can be a real pain because whatever I want to wear is *always* in the other apartment.'

A black and white electric guitar lay propped up against the wall beside Finn's bed. I reached out to touch it.

'Don't touch that!' said Greg quickly. 'Finn will go crazy.'

I withdrew my hand at once.

'Evie, do you want me to come with you to Brooklyn to speak to Sidney?' Greg asked.

'No, I think it would be better if I spoke to her without you guys. Jake and Scott are going to some car-racing event in Delaware on Saturday afternoon. So that's my best chance of catching Sidney at home.'

Dr Pepper scuttled under Greg's bed at the knock on the door.

'The pizza is here, guys. Come into the kitchen to eat.'

'Thanks, Mrs Winters,' said Kylie, carefully waiting until I had shoved our masterpiece script into my backpack before opening the door.

'I'm using my maiden name again now. It's Angela Rackett, but you can call me Angela, honey. Hearing "Mrs Rackett" makes me look over my shoulder to see if my mother is standing there with her broomstick,' and she laughed to herself.

Greg rolled his eyes but in more of an affectionate than an exasperated way. I explained that Scott was nearby in Angela's East Village neighbourhood visiting an off-colour Dalmatian owned by the local firehouse and would pick me up after lunch.

'Off-colour?' asked Greg. 'Has the Dalmatian lost his spots?'

'No, I don't think so,' I said, 'I don't think spots can be lost.'

Scott arrived after lunch and after spending a few minutes charming Angela, he suggested we take the subway home because his Jeep was being temperamental again. We took the 6 subway line at 23rd Street to the 86th Street Station, intending to walk the rest of the way home through the Park. I glanced in the window of the pet gym on the corner of East 87th and Lexington Avenue. A tired-looking iguana was running on a miniature treadmill.

'Only in New York would somebody pay fifty bucks an hour because they think their pet iguana looks fat,' said Scott, shaking his head in wonder and disgust.

'It's Charley!' I said and I rapped on the window.

The sudden noise prompted Charley to try to jump off the treadmill, but he was attached to it by his leash. He ended up nearly hanging himself until Eliot ran over and disentangled him.

'Sorry,' I mouthed through the glass.

'Let's get out of here,' said Scott, tugging on my hood.

On Saturday morning after Scott and Jake had left, I told Joanna that I had something important to do and asked if it would be ok if I didn't help out in the clinic.

'What do you have to do?' she asked curiously.

'It's personal,' I told her.

'Ok,' she said in a moderately hurt way and didn't ask any more questions.

I eventually found Sidney's apartment after getting directions from a woman pushing a stroller in Williamsburg. Sidney answered the apartment intercom buzzer after a minute or two. She sounded surprised when she heard who it was. But she buzzed the front door open right away and said, 'Come on up, we're on the top floor, it's a walk-up. Katie's having a nap so try and be quiet when you reach the apartment.'

I slid through the door and headed for the stairs, which were very narrow and grimy. There was lots of thinking time, climbing five flights of stairs.

Later that day, I lay full length on my stomach on my bed, trying to read *David Copperfield*, which Mrs Scanlon had given to me as a goodbye present. I suppose she thought I would have something in common with David, since he was an orphan and I am effectively an orphan. I thought David was a bit wimpy and whiny even if he did have a monster stepfather and a selfish, cowardly mother. There were lots of long difficult parts to skip over. I tossed the book aside.

I stared at the spidery crack in the corner of the ceiling that had started to spread. Like a virus, I thought, because that was the mood I was in. Leela's words kept spinning around in my head. I remembered Grainne, from my old class at school in Dublin, who got her ponytail caught in the blender when her mum was whipping cream. I felt like my whole head was caught in a blender. How dare Leela speak about my mum the way she did? But I felt furious with Mum too. Why did she leave me as a financial burden on Uncle Scott? She should have bought life insurance. She was always talking about getting a policy, but I guess she never got around to it.

I hate being a financial drain on Scott, sucking up all his cash like a Hoover. If only I lived back in Jane Eyre's time: I could train to become a governess and teach little rich children how to do their ABCs. That is what penniless girl orphans did in those days. Nowadays, in the books, they all are wizards or werewolves or half-fairies, or they are recruited by friendly pirates or adopted by a gay couple or a celebrity. Practical help is sadly wanting.

I feel guilty for being angry with Mum when she is dead. Janet said that Mum is always with me, looking down on me from heaven. I hope Mum is having fun and is happy and not wasting her days in heaven watching me – that would be terribly boring.

Is Leela right? Am I causing Scott to go bankrupt? I know he had to use his overdraft account at the bank to pay Karen last week. And I heard him on the phone asking someone from our building's management company for extra time to pay this month's rent on the apartment. At least the rent on the clinic has been paid … I hope.

The only person Scott is afraid of is Virpi, the Finnish chain-smoking bookkeeper who arrives on the last Thursday of every month to trawl through the invoices with him. She has a habit every ten minutes or so of breaking into hysterical laughter over some of the receipts and expenses, culminating in a bone-rattling cough, during which she drops ash on Scott's Italian shoes. Virpi is the only person I have met who is totally immune to Scott's charm. He doesn't like it one little bit. He thinks she might be an alien who has taken over a human body and is planning the destruction of the human race. I think he's only half-joking.

I explained Scott's theory to Kylie and Greg. She thought it was funny but Greg said he didn't think an enemy alien would spend so much time doing Scott's bookkeeping.

The more I think about it the more I become convinced that Leela was right. It would be best for Scott if I return to Ireland. I will go back and live with Janet and Brendan (if Brendan is still in the picture) and go back to school. Scott will probably call me; we will exchange Christmas and birthdays gifts, but soon that will fade out. Joanna will forget about me and Kylie and Greg will forget too and I will never see Finn again and I will never give Luna a carrot or groom her again and I will sleep all alone by myself, not with Ben's head on my foot and I won't hear him snoring or the exciting little yapping noises he makes when he is chasing squirrels in his dreams and it will be like this summer never happened.

I must have fallen asleep, because the next thing, I heard laughter and loud voices. Jake and Scott had arrived back from the car races in high spirits and in time for Joanna to take me, Kylie and Greg to a Yankees game in Yankee Stadium in the Bronx. I wandered out to the living room, feeling more cheerful. Stefan was supposed to come with us, but Joanna said Rachel would be taking his ticket.

'Trouble in paradise?' Scott inquired.

'No,' snapped Joanna, 'and by the way, Adrienne Weismann called. She has diagnosed KitKat with one of her makey-upey diseases. She particularly wants to discuss it with you. I told her you would love to hear all about her diagnosis and that you will call her this evening.'

Scott cursed. It was not a mild curse.

I enjoyed the Yankees game although Greg gave up trying to explain the rules of baseball to me. The hot dogs were the best part. I have never tasted such delicious hot dogs in my life. We all ate two each. Kylie ate hers with just ketchup; Greg mixed mustard and ketchup and loaded it with sauerkraut. I liked them best with plain mustard.

Joanna was not herself, but we were all too cautious to comment on it.

'What's up with you, Joanna?' Rachel finally asked.

'Stefan and I broke up.'

Kylie and I looked up. This was more interesting than the game.

'I'm sorry, Jo,' said Rachel.

'Don't be,' Joanna replied, 'it's been coming for a while.'

Rachel looked confused.

'I thought you were so happy with him. What happened?'

Joanna shrugged.

'I pretended to everyone and to myself that I was happy with him. I don't know why. I wanted to be happy and he was European and sophisticated, and I don't know, I think I was fed up with dating, with speed dating events and meeting lots of Bengali taxi drivers. I'm sure they were very nice but I don't have a word of Bengali.'

Rachel laughed and Joanna scowled at her.

'I'm sorry you are upset,' I said.

'That's ok, Evie, no loss,' said Joanna.

'I hated Stefan's big gorilla feet,' added Rachel with a little shudder.

'Let the trashing begin!' said Joanna in a sarcastic tone and we all took the hint to change the subject.

On our way home on the jam-packed subway, I had my first opportunity to speak to Kylie and Greg without adults around since my trip to Brooklyn that morning. Rachel and Joanna managed to grab seats and were embroiled in conversation. Greg, Kylie and I were squashed together by the doors.

'What did Sidney say?' Greg asked as soon as he could.

I hadn't been looking forward to this conversation, especially considering all the efforts Kylie and Greg had put into the script.

'Em,' I said, 'I didn't actually ask her to do it.'

'You chickened out?' asked Kylie.

Greg looked disbelieving.

'No way did I *chicken* out. I just changed my mind about the plan.'

'It was so complicated,' I pointed out, my words tumbling over one another in my rush. 'We had to persuade Sidney to let us use her studio to set up the bogus audition … and where were we going to find a beehive? … and what if Scott didn't turn up at the right time? … or what if Leela just called that TV producer guy and realised that the audition was not real? … and what if the bees didn't swarm out of their hive when they were supposed to? … and …'

'Ok,' said Greg, the chief writer, a little huffily, 'so we have some revisions to do. I wasn't totally comfortable with the whole bee aspect of the script. I mean, I could probably attract a mosquito bite at the Arctic pole, so being around a hive of bees probably wasn't the smartest idea.'

I shook my head.

'It's not just the bees. Janet, my godmother, would say that we are living in *la la land*. I thought about it the whole time when I was climbing up the stairs to Sidney's apartment, which took forever, and I thought about it all the way back from Brooklyn. *I have to use my words.* I have to confront Leela directly.'

Greg did not seem impressed.

'Now, that sounds *ley la land* to me.'

'It's *la la land*,' I pointed out.

'Whatever.'

Kylie stuck her tongue out at Greg.

'I think Evie is right. Our plan was kids' stuff. Leela is real.'

'Guys,' called Joanna, 'hurry up, we've reached our stop.'

I forgot to tell Sidney not to tell anyone that I had dropped in to see her. She told Jake, who told Scott. When I got home from the Yankees game, Scott was not remotely interested in hearing about it. He was icy cold, which I hate more than anything. It is so much easier to deal with someone who is yelling.

'I cannot *believe* you went out to Williamsburg on your own. I thought I could trust you. I thought you didn't want to be treated like a little kid. Now I'm going to have to keep tabs on you, maybe I'll have to get one of those microchips we put in the dogs and cats and implant it in your elbow. Is that what you want?'

I stared at the floor.

'Why did you go to Brooklyn without asking me?'

I didn't say anything. Scott waited. Still, I said nothing.

'Alright, here's the deal,' said Scott. 'You are not going to your riding lesson tomorrow or next Sunday either.'

'NO!' I wailed. 'Couldn't we substitute an alternative punishment, like I have to clean out the kennels every day or ...?'

'No, we can't! There will be no substitutions. Maybe this will help you to realise that there are bad people out there. When I told you that you always have to tell me where you are going and who you are with, I was not kidding around.'

'But Scott,' I said, 'Luna will be devastated when I don't turn up.'

'Well, you should have thought about Luna before you went wandering around Brooklyn by yourself,' he said unsympathetically.

That was the end of it and it left me seething with rage. Adults are always saying stuff that doesn't make any sense. Since it would never have occurred to me that Scott could be so cruel as to ban me from riding Luna, I couldn't *possibly* have thought about that before going to Brooklyn.

Chapter 23

Not including stuff to do with Mum, today was the saddest day of my life so far. It started off like a normal day: breakfast, a walk in the Park with Ben, some banter with Frank about which local deli has the best bagels. When I returned to the apartment, Joanna was making coffee and talking to Scott about a pug with heartworm disease as he threw items into his blue workbag.

'Where are you going, Scott? Can I come?'

'Not this one, Evie. I'm going to see a very sick cat at a shelter way uptown. Why don't you help out in the clinic this morning?'

'Tommy is coming in for a check-up. I could use an extra set of hands,' Joanna chipped in.

I wavered. I was very fond of Tommy, an enormous, dignified Airedale, but I'd met him several times.

'Karen could help Joanna. I've never been to an animal shelter. Please, Scott?'

He hesitated.

'No point in over *sheltering* Evie,' suggested Joanna with a wink at me.

Scott groaned.

'You guys are killing me. Anything for a peaceful life. Jump to it, Evie!'

The shelter was located in a warehouse in a derelict section of Washington Heights, a residential neighbourhood above Harlem in Manhattan. Hundreds of wire-mesh crates and kennels lined almost every centimetre of space, many of them containing more than one dog or cat crammed in together. The normal luxuries I had come to associate with Manhattan pets – plush pet toys, customised blankets, doggie beds, tennis balls and exotic biscuit and cupcake treats – were nowhere to be seen. These animals had water and the cheapest kind of dry kibble; that was all.

I trailed Scott slowly through the warehouse. I couldn't hear what he was saying to Miriam, the shelter supervisor, because of the terrific din caused by so many barking dogs. But it wasn't the noisy dogs that caught my eye; it was the ones lying morosely at the very back of their crates without making a sound, not even a whimper. They didn't care enough to lift their heads as we passed.

I stopped in front of a crate containing a medium-sized, shaggy dog with matted ginger and brown fur. I slipped my hand through the bars of the crate to encourage her to approach for a pat, but she strained back even further, pressing up against the bars at the back of the crate, looking at me with terribly sad, frightened and bewildered brown eyes.

'I won't hurt you,' I said, horrified.

'What's this dog's name?' I called up to Miriam.

'Two-Forty-Seven,' she answered, consulting a clipboard

and shaking her head. 'We got so many new dogs this past week that we haven't had the time yet to clean them all, much less give them names.'

No loving owner, no toys, no treats, no name.

I fished in my pocket and pulled out a small handful of Ben's bacon bits treats, wrapped in cling film. I pulled off the plastic, got down on my knees and pushed the bacon through the bars.

'You look like a Lindsey, you just do. Here, Lindsey, treat for you, girl.'

Lindsey eyed the snack suspiciously, but after a few minutes, she roused herself, approached cautiously and sniffed at my outstretched hand. Soon she gobbled the treats down. I put my hand very slowly through the bars again to touch her, but she retreated to the back of the crate again.

'Bye, Lindsey,' I whispered, 'you're a *good* dog,' and I rushed to catch up with Scott and Miriam. They were discussing a large, skeleton-skinny, striped black and white cat, which lay in Miriam's arms. Scott rubbed the cat gently and spoke softly to Miriam.

'It's too late. I'm sorry. It will just be a few minutes,' he said, as he gave the cat an injection.

'At least she's not dying alone, poor Sebbie,' said Miriam and she lowered her large, bulky body onto the concrete floor, the cat still carefully cradled in her arms, and waited for death to come.

'Did she say Sebbie?" I asked Scott.

'No. Zebbie, for zebra,' he answered, indicating the black

and white stripes.

Zebra's breath, which had been a rasping sound, stopped and it fell silent in the shelter as if all the other dogs and cats were mourning for a moment. I turned and walked away quickly, past Lindsey, past the assorted abandoned dogs and cats and into sunlight so bright white that it hurt my eyes and made them water. I waited for Scott by his jeep. When he came out, he didn't say anything. He just opened up the car door for me and we drove off down Frederick Douglass Boulevard towards home.

Scott switched the radio on. A presenter was interviewing a filmmaker about a documentary he had directed on the American civil war.

'We had a civil war in Ireland a long time ago,' I said to Scott, 'and Michael Collins got shot dead.'

'In the head,' I added.

'I saw the Liam Neeson film about it,' Scott replied.

We stayed quiet for a while, but anger seethed through me.

'How can people do it?' I said, loudly. 'How can they be so cruel to hurt and abandon helpless animals like that?'

'I don't know, Evie,' said Scott. 'But you have to think about the good guys, people like Miriam. She works tirelessly day and night for those animals; she tries to do as much as she can and that's a lot. She lobbied relentlessly for a decade to get that warehouse donated for free and she has a whole army of volunteers who help. They feed the animals, clean them, exercise them, find them foster homes and forever homes too. Wait until you see, when we go back there next month, Miriam and her helpers will have found forever homes for many of those dogs and cats, maybe even for your ginger dog friend.'

'Lindsey,' I said. 'What will happen to her if they don't find her a forever home? She won't get put down, will she?'

'No. Not at Miriam's shelter, it's a no-kill shelter. Eventually, she will find a good home for her. We can ask Miriam about Lindsey the next time we visit. You can bring some of Ben's extra toys and help out.'

'Yes, I can do that. I would love to help,' I said, and then I remembered, 'but I won't be here. I'm going back to Ireland soon.'

Scott did not ignore this as he usually does.

'Really?' he said, in an exasperated voice.

I felt a lump in my throat.

'Yes,' I croaked.

'Look, Evie, we did ok, didn't we? I mean, you seem happy. I love you. Joanna loves you. Stay with us. We're not a traditional family and I'm not saying we're perfect, but we are a family – you, me, Ben, our patients, their owners.'

I didn't know what to say, because I realised with as much certainty as I knew my own name that I wanted to stay. But there is no way I wanted to be a big, money-sucking leech.

'I love you too, all of you, but I want to go home to Ireland,' I whispered.

Scott sighed.

'Why don't you just go for a little vacation to see Janet and David and your friends and come back here before you miss too much school,' he suggested.

He added, 'Staying here with us does not mean giving up Ireland or being Irish. You can spend your holidays there in the summer.'

'No!' I said. 'You promised I could go back to Ireland at the end of the summer. It's nearly the end of the summer.'

'I don't want to stay here,' I added forcefully.

I glanced at Scott's profile. But he can be as good at masking feelings as I am.

'Yes, I promised. You are as stubborn as your mother. You want to leave, leave. I'll get your airline ticket tonight.'

'Thank you,' I said stiffly in a small voice, but he didn't reply.

Neither of us said a single word the rest of the way home.

When we got back, Scott rushed off to shower and change because he and Leela were going to some fancy charity ball tonight in midtown.

I was hanging out in the living room, channel surfing, when Leela swept in, wearing a long, sleek, strapless, red-orange dress and satin slippers, with glittering jewels in her hair. She looked stunningly beautiful, like a character from *The Arabian Nights*. I didn't give her the satisfaction of telling her that. I've been finding it very difficult even to look at her since I overheard her phone call to Kirsten.

'How do I look?' she asked me, twirling around.

'Fine,' I said begrudgingly.

She teetered off down the hallway to seek a more satisfactory answer from Scott, who, dressed in his tuxedo, looked very like James Bond.

Chapter 24

The man sitting next to an orange and yellow snake in a crate was reading a comic book when I entered the waiting room. I stopped abruptly. I had no experience with snakes at all so this could be a good opportunity to learn something about them. The snake seemed to be sleeping. I took the seat on other side of the man, not beside the crate.

'What's your snake's name?' I asked politely.

'Willie,' he said, in a Scottish accent.

'And what's your name?'

'Willie,' he said, a little louder, in a defensive tone.

I noticed that Willie's hair was almost exactly the same shade of orange as the markings on reptilian Willie.

'What does he eat?' I asked.

'I buy him frozen mice every week.'

Uugh, I thought.

'He loves them. He's a corn snake. He doesn't look it because he's all curled up, but he is nearly as long as you are.'

'What's wrong with your snake?' interrupted Mr Fannelli from three seats down, where he was waiting for Scott to finish with Spike.

'Spike got into a gallon of pickles this time, Miss Evie,' he added.

Willie, the man, said, 'My snake has a respiratory problem.'

Mr Fannelli looked puzzled.

'How can you tell if a snake has a respiratory problem?' he wondered.

'Because, normally, when he hisses it sounds like this, *sssssss, sssssss* and now when he hisses, it sounds like this, *SHHHHHHHHH, SHHHHHHHHHH* and he makes little clicking noises and sometimes he coughs.'

On cue, Willie coughed.

Mr Fannelli regarded both Willies silently for a few moments.

Then he said, 'Well, a lot of people would say only freaks keep pet snakes, but I say if snakes are your hobby, that's your hobby and that's fine so long as you don't let it get out and poison someone or their dog.'

Willie looked like he would probably punch Mr Fannelli if he were not an old man.

'He's not a venomous snake,' he said, through gritted teeth.

Mr Fannelli smiled, oblivious of having caused offence.

Karen called out, 'Willie, Dr Brooks will see Willie now.'

'Good luck!' said Mr Fannelli.

Willie hissed at him, Willie the snake, that is, not Willie the man.

I slipped into the examining room right behind them and took up a position beside the door well behind Scott, but with a good view of the table.

'He's got very handsome markings,' said Scott, and Willie blushed with pride.

Scott opened the lid of the crate and, taking the snake's head between his thumb and fingers, eased him out onto the table. The snake didn't seem to mind. I watched the snake as Scott examined him and talked to Willie about his symptoms.

'Just a minor infection,' he decided. 'Raise the temperature in his enclosure and give me a call if you don't see any signs of improvement in a few days.'

Willie leaned down and kissed Willie on his head. It was very cute in a have-to-be-there-to-believe-it kind of way.

Joanna was off the next day because she had swapped days with Scott. She said that she needed to have Tuesday off to do something. She didn't tell Scott or me any more than that. But when I mentioned this to Kylie while we hung out in her bedroom, Kylie said that she knew what Joanna was doing.

'She's having laser surgery on her eyes, so she will have nearly perfect eyesight and won't need to wear glasses anymore. My mom is picking her up at the doctor's office at three o'clock because her eyes will be bandaged and she will be all doped up. She has to go straight to bed and sleep right through until tomorrow morning.'

'Poor, poor Joanna,' I said. 'She should have told us. Surgery! And on her eyes! That sounds scary. I hope she's going to be ok.'

Kylie nodded reassuringly.

'People do laser surgery all the time. Mom's sister, my aunt Odile, used to be practically blind without her glasses, and after her laser surgery, she had Superman vision,' she said.

I still felt worried as I walked home through the Park. Later that afternoon, I helped Scott with a check-up for a Siamese cat whose owner was moving with him to Singapore and needed a veterinary export certificate. Just as Scott finished signing the certificate, his cell phone rang. It was Rachel in a state of panic.

'Whoa!' said Scott. 'Calm down and tell me the problem.'

'I was supposed to pick up Joanna at three. She's having laser surgery. I'm not supposed to tell anyone. But now I have a huge problem at the gallery and I can't get away.'

'No problem,' said Scott. 'I'll get Joanna, just give me the address.'

'Tell Jo I am so sorry,' said Rachel, and she called out the doctor's Park Avenue address.

Scott left Karen and me in charge of the clinic, which was quite a big responsibility.

'I don't want you doing any operations without me unless they are necessary,' he joked with us. 'Reschedule all the appointments and send any walk-ins to Peter's clinic on Sixty-Second.'

I wandered aimlessly back and forth between the waiting room and the examining room, hoping very hard that Joanna's surgery was going ok. A fat man with a red-brown moustache came into the clinic carrying a bowl of tropical fish and asked Karen if he could see the vet.

'The vets are all out,' said Karen.

'Can I help you?' I asked in a professional tone, wishing that I was at the other side of Karen's desk, because it was such a tall desk, only my head appeared at the top.

The man did a double take.

'Who are you? Doogie Howser?' he asked.

'Em, no, I don't know who that is,' I said. 'My uncle's the vet here and I've been helping him all summer so maybe I could take a look at your fish, although I haven't had a lot of experience with fish and even the two goldfish I had, they both died, but I could give it a go.'

The man shrank back, clutching his fish bowl as if I had proposed poisoning his pets.

'I must have mixed up my meds again,' he said, more to himself than to me and Karen and, with a flurry of apologies, he backed out the door.

'We can't help those who don't want to be helped,' said Karen.

About an hour later, I heard footsteps overhead and dashed upstairs to the apartment to see Scott leading Joanna by the hand around the furniture. She wore big goggles over her bandaged eyes.

'Hi, Joanna, are you ok? Did it hurt?' I asked, as I took her other hand.

'Nope, I didn't feel any pain and with the quantity of painkillers and sleeping pills in my system, I don't expect to feel anything.'

She giggled a little.

Scott and I walked her into his bedroom. She began to protest. 'I'm not taking your room, Scott. Really, I will be fine by myself in my own apartment.'

'And how do you plan on getting there?' he asked sarcastically.

'Just bring me downstairs and hail me a cab,' she said.

'Stop talking, Joanna, or I will get into bed with you myself to make you stay there.'

'Oh!' said Joanna, and then, in a small voice, 'I have a bag with my stuff.'

'I'll get it,' I said, and quickly found it on the kitchen counter and brought it into Scott's bedroom.

'I can undress myself,' Joanna insisted. 'I want to sleep for a few centuries.'

'I'll stay with her until she gets into bed,' I told Scott.

'Has he gone?' asked Joanna.

I nodded and then remembered that she couldn't see me.

'Yes,' I spoke up. 'You can get undressed now and into your PJs. Let me help you.'

After Joanna was in bed, Scott came in to check on her.

'Good night. Sleep well!' he said, 'and in the morning, you will finally be able to appreciate how good looking I really am.'

'Go away!' she said in a very sleepy, but amused voice.

Ben jumped up on the bed and positioned himself comfortably by her feet.

'Get down, Ben,' said Scott.

'No, leave him here,' said Joanna, feeling around with her arms to find him for a pat.

Scott and I quietly left the room.

Chapter 25

I looked up from my Friday morning pancakes at the diner to see what had caught Scott's attention outside. It was Joanna passing the window on the way to join us for breakfast. A minute later, she slipped into the booth beside me, said 'good morning!' without making eye contact, and buried herself in her menu. It was obvious why Scott had been staring. Joanna was dressed in a flirty, wispy, pale yellow summer dress with spaghetti straps.

'What induced you to come out of regulation black?' Scott asked. 'We've just got used to seeing you without glasses.'

Joanna looked uncomfortable. She lowered her menu, raised her chin and sat up straighter insofar as you can sit up straight on the sagging, stained-red cushion covering on the booth bench.

'I'm thirty-three. I have not worn anything but black in nearly fifteen years. I thought maybe it was time for a change.'

'I like it,' said Scott. 'Colour suits you.'

'You look fantastic,' I added.

It was a slow morning at the clinic. Janet telephoned at lunchtime to find out what date I was heading back to Dublin.

'I'll check,' I told her.

I hung around Scott all afternoon, waiting for, and dreading, the right opportunity. Finally, he got exasperated when he bumped into me because I was standing so close behind him.

'That's the third time I've nearly stood on your feet. What's up, Evie? What are you doing following me around?'

I thought best just to come right out with it.

'Janet wants to know when I am going back to Ireland.'

'I bought your ticket,' he said.

'You did?'

'Yes, it's for September third,' he said, curtly.

'Thanks,' I said.

'You're welcome. Could you go see if we have more Frontline on the second shelf in the waiting room, that's the tick worm medication.'

'Ok.'

We didn't discuss my flight again. I sent a text to Kylie and Greg, explaining that I was leaving on September third, which left us just over a week to implement a plan to get rid of Leela.

As I was waiting for a response, I noticed an unpleasant, strong, musty urine smell in the waiting room and I looked around. A man with a little boy and a small, brown and white animal that looked a bit like a monkey wearing dark sunglasses, looked at me apologetically.

'What is that?' I asked.

'A meerkat,' the man said, 'very smelly when they go to the bathroom.'

Scott came into the waiting room and shook hands with the man.

'Hi Rob, how are you doing?'

'How about those Mets?' Rob answered and they launched into a baseball conversation.

I sat down beside the cute, curly haired little boy.

'What's your name?' I asked.

'Harry,' he said. 'My teacher says I am "Handsome Harry". I have a brother, Toby, but he is called "Tobes". He can't talk. He's just a baby.'

'How old are you?'

He held up four fingers.

'What's your meerkat called?'

'Spiderman,' he answered.

His dad turned and looked at him.

'Harry, you know his name is Zak.' He explained to Scott, 'he's going through a real Spiderman stage. It's been going on for over a year now. My wife and I get down on our knees every night and pray he will switch to Batman, just for a change.'

'Who is our President?' Scott asked Harry.

'Spiderman,' he said, confidently.

'See what I mean,' said his dad.

When Scott lifted Zak out of his cage, I noticed he had only four toes on each foot, or would you call it a paw? I'm not sure.

'Where do meerkats come from?' I asked.

'The Kalahari Desert in Africa,' Rob answered.

Scott sat Zak on the scales.

'One and a half pounds,' he noted, writing it into his chart. Rob showed Scott photographs of the large, special enclosure he and his brother-in-law had built in his big backyard in Long Island for Zak.

'What made you buy a meerkat?' I wondered.

'Harry drove me and his mom crazy after he saw the *Lion King* movie. There's a meerkat character in the movie called Timon. I suppose we're lucky he didn't want a Simba.'

Scott sighed.

'The *Lion King* producers have a lot to answer for. I've had so many Manhattan parents buying meerkats and trying to keep them in their pokey little apartments. Then, of course, they want to dump them when they realise meerkats are completely unsuited for apartment living.'

'Zak loves digging,' Harry announced, 'and he likes lying around all day sunbathing like Mommy.'

Rob and Scott laughed.

'I wouldn't let your mom hear you say that, buddy,' said Rob.

Scott had finished his examination. I could tell he didn't have a clue what was ailing Zak.

'Give me a minute,' he asked Rob and he went off to make a telephone call. He was back a few minutes later.

'Rob, I'm not an expert in meerkats. I can't figure out what's wrong with the little guy. I want you to take Zak to my friend, Dr Shin in New Jersey, who specialises in meerkats and other exotic pets. Karen will give you her address.'

'Thanks,' said Rob. 'What do I owe you?'

Scott shook his head.

'No charge. I couldn't help. Give me a call and let me know how it goes with Dr Shin.'

'Sure,' said Rob, lifting Zak back in his cage.

'Phewsh, phewsh,' said Harry, putting out both his upturned wrists towards Scott and shooting him with imaginary webs.

'Phewsh, phewsh,' said Scott, spinning around and getting him back.

Karen walked in, holding a clipboard.

'I've got a Mr Garvey with a giant Schnauzer for you, Dr Brooks, and he says he cannot wait any longer.'

'Send him in,' said Scott, and we said goodbye to Rob, Harry and Zak.

'Rob is the attorney I used when I leased this place,' Scott told me, 'a good guy'.

Mr Garvey was about fifty years old. He was dressed in a dark pinstriped suit and he strode into the examining room as if he owned the place, talking on his BlackBerry.

'Excuse me,' he said to whoever he was talking to, and he said to Scott, 'This is Hooter,' pointing at the dog. 'He is driving me and my girlfriend and all our neighbours crazy with his barking. The building Coop is sending me nasty letters. I need you to debark him,' and he began talking into his BlackBerry again, before Scott had a chance to speak.

Scott looked at Mr Garvey as if he were an axe murderer.

'We don't do debarking here,' he said shortly, opening the door pointedly for Mr Garvey to leave. I felt so sorry for

Hooter, who looked like a really nice dog. Mr Garvey paused his telephone conversation.

'I've just waited for nearly twenty minutes. I don't have time to go to another vet. What's the big deal? It's my dog and if I want it debarked, that's my right, so just do your job and we can all get on with our lives.'

'We don't believe in robbing dogs of their voices for their owners' convenience,' said Scott, in his deadly, quiet, low voice. 'Now, you're wasting my time as well as your own, so I suggest you get moving.'

Mr Garvey slung the BlackBerry into a pouch at the side of his waist.

'Tell me what vet around here does debarking.'

'I don't know,' said Scott.

'Yeah, right, I bet you don't,' the man sneered. 'Who do you think you are, Doctor Doolittle or something?'

Scott said, 'I will give *you* five seconds to get out of here but you can leave Hooter here and I will find a good home for him and his bark.'

Mr Garvey looked like he was going to say something, but thought better of it. Even wearing his professional white coat, Scott looks like the kind of guy who knows how to throw a punch. Mr Garvey strode out of the examining room, muttering under his breath and dragging a very reluctant Hooter with him.

'Can you call the police, Scott, to rescue Hooter so that man does not get his voice box removed?' I asked.

'I wish I could, Evie, but debarking is not illegal. He will find a vet to do the job.'

'But that's terrible,' I said. 'We have to stop it.'

'Evie, we can't do anything. Let's concentrate on the animals we can help, ok?'

'Ok,' I said. But it was not okay as far as I was concerned. I can imagine how Ben would feel if his bark was taken away. He would be miserable. Poor Hooter.

I saw Kylie and Camille in the evening because Camille's mom took us to watch an outdoor opera at the Great Lawn in Central Park. People and blankets and picnic baskets took up every inch of the lawn. Camille's mom forced her way through the crowds and shamelessly opened up her lawn chair on top of a teenage couple's blanket. She ignored their outraged faces, beckoning to us to sit on the grass beside her. We were so far from the stage that I couldn't make out the individual faces of the members of the orchestra, just their shadowy outlines. They started to tune up and a hush of anticipation fell over the crowd.

'I can't believe all these thousands of New Yorkers are keeping quiet,' said Kylie.

'Sssh,' said Camille's mom.

We talked in whispers after that.

Camille told us that she spends every weekend at her parents' summer home on the beach in the Hamptons. When she found out that neither Kylie nor I had summer homes in the Hamptons, she raised her eyebrows so high that they disappeared beneath her hair.

'That's so weird,' she said, wrinkling her button nose and

giving a little laugh. 'We had such fun last weekend. My cousins, Tamara and Coltan, came to hang out by our pool on Sunday. Tamara brought her boyfriend, Finn. You guys know him, right?'

'A little,' I said.

'Oh, I think he knows you more than a little,' Camille snickered. 'He said he doesn't like girls like you who think too much.'

I felt like she had stabbed me in the stomach with a giant pair of rusty scissors. There was no way that Camille could be lying. *You think a lot*, I remember Finn had said to me.

Camille continued.

'You can tell Finn is so crazy about Tamara – she is a goddess and so intelligent, she gets straight As all the time.'

'There's a very big difference between being intelligent and "thinking too much",' she added.

Kylie, looking at my face, interjected.

'I think too much!' she said loudly. 'Way too much. I think too much all the time. In fact, I am thinking too much right now and, Camille, can you guess what I am thinking too much about this very second?'

Rising to a kneeling position, she stared down at Camille with withering contempt gleaming in her eyes. Camille turned her head away and began to apply lip-gloss.

'Whatever. I'm not going to be one of those girls that bores boys to death by thinking too much.'

I felt like crawling under the teenage couple's blanket in shame and embarrassment.

Chapter 26

The forecast for Saturday predicted thunderstorms, but I woke to a cloudless sky. Angela and her new boyfriend, Leonard, had hired a minivan to take me, Kylie, Greg, Finn, Tamara, her twin brother Coltan and Finn's friend, Akono, to Six Flags Great Adventure in Jackson, New Jersey — an amazing amusement park with tons of roller coasters and rides. I sat wedged between Kylie and Akono during the long drive, very glad that I did not have to sit beside Finn or Coltan. I intensely disliked Coltan as soon as I met him. He looks like Tamara, but has a floppy fringe and none of her sweetness. Everyone bores him. I can't understand why Kylie likes him. When I got the chance to ask her, she shrugged and said, 'Everyone wants to hang out with Coltan.'

'Not me,' I said.

Akono is one of Finn's best friends. He is tall with very black skin. He told me that both his parents are doctors who immigrated to New York from Lagos in Nigeria before he was born. Akono has visited Nigeria five times to see his grandparents and other relatives. He listened very attentively to the 'Hooter' story and said that he was thinking about becoming a vet and would like to meet Scott.

I said, 'Sure, I'll ask Scott.'

Finn said, 'Someone should take a hockey stick to Hooter's owner's head.'

I ignored him. I have no space in my head for Finn Winters, particularly because my head is obviously already too full of thoughts.

'No, man,' protested Akono. 'That is not the solution. Some people are always too quick to fight.'

'And some people are never quick enough,' responded Finn, but in a teasing tone. Akono laughed.

Greg doesn't like Leonard because he is still in his late thirties and Greg thinks he is far too young to be dating his mom. Greg told me that Angela has been forty-nine for five years in a row now. Leonard works as a stand-up comic in a little club downtown. He is trying to break into the big clubs and into television. During the drive on the New Jersey turnpike, he tried out some of his new material on us, but none of it was funny. It was almost embarrassing. Kylie was the only one who laughed now and again. This was not because she is stupid; Kylie is one of the smartest people I know, but she laughed at Leonard's jokes because she has a big heart.

Leonard said, 'You guys are not getting the material because it's adult stuff.'

'Yes, that's the reason,' Greg whispered from behind me.

Leonard told a lot of jokes about how he feels being a fat guy, but his comedy routine had a major glitch because although he had a little beer belly, you couldn't say he was overweight.

Great Adventure was not nearly as much fun as I had hoped because all of the best rides have a height requirement. When you get to the top of the line, you have to stand in front of a measuring tree picture and if you don't reach the red mark, then no matter how much pleading you do, they won't let you on the ride. This kept happening over and over to Greg and me. He seemed to take it more personally. Kylie hit the mark without even standing on her tippy toes.

Greg and I got totally fed up of waiting on lines only to face rejection and so we spent most of the day swimming in the tidal wave pool. Leonard was more excited about the rides than anyone else. He had highlighted a route to the best rides, based on an assessment of the lines on the park map and took charge of herding all the normal-sized people in our group along the route. Angela lay under an enormous blue and white striped umbrella on a lounger beside the tidal pool, and when we swam near her, she yelled over to us that she was sure we would be tall enough to get on the rides next summer. Greg said there wasn't a single kid in the pool that didn't hear her. I won't be around next year, but I didn't bother reminding her of that.

I forgot to be careful when getting back into the car that evening, so I wound up sitting between Finn and the window. I stared out of the window instead of talking to him, although he didn't seem to notice. We all fell asleep on the ride back, except for Leonard who was driving. When I woke up as we crossed the George Washington Bridge into the city, I realised my head was on Finn's shoulder, which was warm, and that I had drooled a little on his t-shirt. I have had many embarrassing moments in my life and this was one of the worst. I said, 'sorry' and he smiled down at me and I smiled back until I remembered I hated him. We reached the Upper West Side first so I got out and Greg came out after me to say goodbye.

'We're running out of time!' he said. 'When did you plan to confront Leela?'

'Soon,' I promised.

Sitting on the floor of my bedroom on Monday morning, I dialled carefully. A bored-sounding, sing-song, female voice answered, 'Lansing, Drucker and Wallis LLP, good morning.'

'Hi,' I said. 'I would like ...' and then I panicked and hung up.

My voice sounded so babyish. It would never do. I gritted my teeth. Mum had been a talented actress and I was her daughter. I could impersonate an adult voice. I dialled the number again. A different, robotic female voice answered. 'Lansing, Drucker and Wallis, good morning.'

'Good morning,' I said, smoothly. 'I would like to schedule an appointment with Miss Leela Patel. It is for ...' but the voice at the other end cut me off abruptly, sounding uninterested.

'Transferring you now,' she said.

Panic coursed through me.

'Good morning. Greta Anderson speaking. How may I assist?'

I felt a rush of relief. I knew who Greta was. Leela had been whining only two weeks ago about having to take her out to lunch for Administrative Assistants' Day. She was Leela's secretary.

'Good morning,' I repeated. 'I would like to schedule an appointment with Miss Patel.'

'You want a consultation?' Greta asked.

'Yes, a consultation, please,' I answered.

'Ms Patel's billing rate for consultations is five hundred and fifty-five dollars per hour.'

There was a pause. Was I supposed to say something?

'Ok,' I said.

'Why are you coming to see Ms Patel?' she asked.

'It's … it's a child-related matter,' I answered. 'About a girl.'

'Custody?' she asked.

'Yes.'

'Has litigation started?'

'I'm not sure,' I said. 'I mean … yes, it just began.'

'If you decide to retain Ms Patel, we will need a signed retainer agreement. The initial retainer fee will be thirty-five thousand dollars. Ms Patel will bring our retainer agreement with her to the consultation.'

Again, there was a pause.

'That works,' I said.

'What's your name and address for our conflict check?'

'Lucy Pensevie,' I answered, saying the first name that came into my head, 'Fifty-four, East 88th Street, Apartment 5L, New York, New York 1024.'

'You are missing a digit in the zip code,' she said.

'Oh yes, sorry, em… 10124.'

'Your telephone number?'

I gave Kylie's cell phone number to her.

'What's the name of the opposing party?'

'Excuse me?' I said.

'Who are you fighting with over the child?'

'Em, the father.'

'What's his name?' she asked in a tone that implied I was a dunce.

'John Donaghy,' I said.

'Can you spell the last name?'

'Sure,' I said and spelled it out. 'The little girl's name is …'

'We don't need the child's name. Ms Patel is free tomorrow morning at 10am. Would that suit?' she asked.

'Yes, fine, thank you.'

'I will call you if there are any problems with the conflict check. Otherwise, we will see you here tomorrow at ten. Our reception is on the forty-first floor. Please remember to bring your chequebook. Goodbye.'

'Bye,' I said, but she had already hung up.

I leaned back against the bed and scratched Ben's ears, feeling both elated and scared. I think I understood why adults are always saying they are stressed.

Chapter 27

A shimmering heat haze blanketed the city early the following morning with still no sign of the long predicted thunderstorm. Even Frank had abandoned his customary cheeriness. I dressed carefully that morning, choosing the navy polka dot dress I had worn to Mum's funeral. It was the only outfit I owned that seemed appropriate. Over it, I put on a white cotton cardigan. I brushed my hair for much longer than usual and then I combed Ben's hair too with a wire-mesh type comb. His nails made a clip-clipping sound on the floor so I took him down to the clinic where Joanna helped me trim his nails. He didn't like it much.

Lucy and Greg walked with me to Leela's office building on Sixth Avenue. We took Ben too because he had a way of making me feel brave. We stood outside the glass turnstile doors, craning our necks to try to see the top of the building.

'Good luck,' said Greg.

'I feel all jangling inside,' said Kylie, 'more nervous than before a skating competition.'

'Let me come with you!' pleaded Greg.

'No, but thank you,' I said. 'You have hockey practice this

morning. And, anyway, one kid is suspicious enough. Two kids would attract too much attention.'

'Text me if you need help,' he said.

I handed over Ben's leash to Kylie.

'I'll wait right here in front of this main entrance,' Kylie said.

I nodded and slipped through the revolving glass doors.

In the middle of the gigantic marble lobby stood a high and narrow desk manned by two security guards. In front of the desk, a line of people waited impatiently. A sign said, 'All Visitors Must Sign In Here.' Nobody took any notice of me as I joined the back of the line. When I reached the top, a fat female security officer barked at me.

'ID.'

I handed over my passport.

'Where are you going?' she asked.

'To see Leela Patel,' I answered.

'What company is she with?'

'Oh, Lansing, Drucker and Wallis.'

I waited for a few seconds as she made a call. I interrupted her, panic-stricken because the company would not have any record of a meeting for Evangeline Brooks.

'I'm joining my stepmom, Lucy Pensevie. She is the one meeting Ms Patel. I forgot something I need for my summer day camp.'

The security guard acted like she didn't hear me, but she said into the phone, 'Lucy Pensevie is meeting Leela Patel this morning. Her stepdaughter, Evangeline, is here. She needs to see her stepmom.'

I felt sweat at the back of my neck drip down my back despite the arctic air conditioning.

'Stand to the left,' the security officer instructed.

I took two steps to the left as a male security guard positioned a tiny camera. Click. He handed me a badge with my photograph on it.

'Forty-first floor,' he said.

I noticed most of the other visitors sticking the badges on their suit jackets. I stuck mine under the collar on the left side of my dress.

I walked towards the first set of elevator banks. There were three electronic barriers and a security guard. I watched two men in grey suits swipe their badges at one of the barriers and walk through. I pulled off my badge and did the same. My triumph was brief because I noticed almost straight away that the elevators only went to the eighteenth floor. I headed back out the barriers.

'Where are you going, kid?' asked the security officer.

'The forty-first floor.'

He pointed across the floor.

'Last elevator bank on the right.'

'Thank you.'

Seven people rode up in the elevator with me – four men and three women. None of them spoke, or looked at me, or at each other. They all tap-tapped rapidly on their BlackBerries, only looking up when it was time to get off at their floors. It was almost like everybody was wearing invisibility cloaks.

Outside the elevators on the forty-first floor were two doors, one for the ladies' restroom and the other for men. Past those doors, two ladies dressed in matching pale blue blouses and navy blue blazers sat behind a reception desk.

'I'm here to see Leela Patel.'

The curly-haired lady looked down at a logbook.

'Where is Mrs Pensevie? Your stepmom, right?'

'Yes, she's just gone into the bathroom,' I said, gesturing behind me, 'and she'll be right out.'

'Ok,' she replied. 'We'll let Ms Patel know you are here. Go ahead and wait in the Thomas Jefferson Conference Room. Take a right at the end of the hallway and it is the first door on your left between the Lincoln and the Roosevelt rooms.'

'Thank you,' I said.

I headed to the conference room. The atmosphere in the law firm was quiet and still like a church. All I could hear was the faint hum of hushed voices. The corridor was lined with vases of artificial flowers and paintings of vases with artificial flowers. I peeped through the open doors of the Ronald Reagan Conference Room. Inside was a long table with at least seventy people in dark suits sitting or standing around it. They had laptops and BlackBerries and stacks of papers in front of them. On the sideboard sat a buffet breakfast spread: bagels, doughnuts, jellies, fruit salad, rye bread, triangular pieces of toast, little plastic tubs of whitefish. I walked quickly past the open doors, found the Jefferson room and pushed open the door. It was much smaller than the Ronald Reagan room, with a table and four chairs in the middle.

On the sideboard, there were bottles of water and soda and a pot of coffee and glasses and china cups and saucers. I took a bottle of water and sat down. Then I decided that could be stealing, so I put it back. I tried each of the chairs and finally decided on the one facing the door. I sat down, put my right hand in the right pocket of my white cotton cardigan and waited.

The door opened and there was a loud gasp.

'Evie! What are *you* doing here?' asked Leela.

'I wanted to talk to you about doing a deal,' I said calmly, as if I visited law firms every day.

'I don't believe this,' she said. 'I don't have time for your little girl games. You have to get out of here right away. I am meeting with a potential client.'

'I *am* Mrs Pensevie,' I said.

'What?'

'I am your potential client.'

'How did you get past security?' she asked.

'That doesn't matter,' I said. 'I want to do a deal with you. I heard what you said to Kirsten on the phone a couple of weeks ago about getting Scott to do that stupid TV show and about how, because of me, Scott is going to go bankrupt.'

'Evie,' she said, folding her arms, 'you are in extremely serious trouble for trespassing like this. If you don't leave right now, I will have to call security to come in here and get you.'

She strode across the room and picked up the phone on the sideboard.

'I don't think you want to do that,' I said quietly. 'There are a lot of very important looking people in the Ronald Reagan room who I'm sure would find it very weird to see a screaming kid dragged past their door by security guards.'

Leela put the phone receiver down with a click, stalked back across the room, shut the door, and stood in front of me.

'What have you got in your pocket?' she said, eyeing my right hand, which still lay in my cardigan pocket.

'Nothing,' I responded.

In an instant, she reached down into my pocket and pulled out a mini tape recorder.

'Evie, Evie,' she said with a fake giggle, 'that is the oldest, most obvious, trick there is.'

I stared down at the mahogany table.

'What do you want?' she asked, putting the recorder carefully in her handbag and sitting down in a black swivel chair across from me.

'I want you to stop trying to get Scott involved in TV programmes. That's all. And if you do that, I won't tell Scott about your stupid plans and I will go back to Ireland on the flight Scott has booked for me.'

Remembering the tagline from a movie trailer, I added, 'Because if you don't, I will be your worst *nightmare.*'

Leela leaned back in her chair and laughed long and hard. She suddenly stopped laughing and snapped, 'Do you know what I do all day long?'

She continued without waiting for an answer.

'I chop little kids like you in half.'

'I will tell you what you are going to do. You are going to keep your mouth shut and get on a plane to Ireland. Because if you tell Scott, guess what? He's not going to believe you anyway. What we have here is a textbook case of step-parent alienation syndrome. I will explain to Scott that you are so jealous of me that you made all that stuff up to try and turn him against me, and Kirsten will back up my story.'

I stayed quiet.

'It's really a very sad syndrome,' she said sweetly. 'Just last month, I represented a mother. We claimed parental aliena-tion, which means that the father deliberately tried to turn the children against my client. And just like that,' she snapped her fingers, 'we got an order from the judge preventing the father from even seeing his own children, except once a month for two hours at Chuck E. Cheese.'

'That's a load of rubbish,' I scoffed. 'Scott's never going to believe that I am alienating him from you. You have no evidence.'

Leela laughed again.

'You are so naïve, sweetie. You don't need *evidence*. You just need to keep repeating the word "syndrome". We could even send you off for evaluation. I have a number of child psy-chologists in my pocket who would be more than happy to write a very damning report about you and your crazy, sad little orphan efforts to alienate Scott from me.'

I stood up, walked to the door and opened it.

'Are you finished?' I asked.

'I think I've said all I needed to say,' she replied, still smiling.

'Good,' I said, and on a stupid, irresistible impulse, I leaned down and pulled a tiny miniature recorder out of my left shoe, 'because I guess that means I can switch this off now.'

Sidney's warning echoed in my head, 'Make sure the big recorder is obvious so when she "finds" it, with any luck it won't occur to her to look for a second.'

Thank you, Sidney, I thought and I didn't wait for Leela's reaction. I ran as fast as I could, down the corridor past the conference rooms and the very surprised-looking reception-ists and out to the elevator banks where a bunch of people were waiting for an elevator. They stared at me, BlackBerries frozen in their hands. I glanced behind and saw that Leela had reached the reception desk. Panicked, I pushed my way through the crowd and pulled open the heavy door under the red neon-lit sign, 'Emergency Staircase'.

It was dark and deathly quiet inside the stairwell but there were emergency light strips on each stair so I could see enough to half-run, half-stumble my way down, clutching the iron railing. Forty. Thirty-Nine. Thirty-Eight. Thirty-Seven. Gasp. Thirty-Six. Thirty-Five. Thirty-Four. Thirty-Three. On the Thirty-Second floor, I halted to catch my breath and to listen for sounds of anyone following me, but I heard nothing. I resumed my downward escape, able to take the flights of stairs faster now that my eyes had adjusted to the semi-darkness, counting each floor as I descended lower and lower. It took about half an hour to reach the second floor, which is when I heard a door opening a floor above me and the sound of quick footsteps and the beam of a torch.

I glanced up to see a brown-haired security guard.

'Evelyn,' he called out in a thick New York accent. 'Stop! Stay where you are.'

I grabbed the handle of the nearest door, yanked it open and continued to run. I found myself in a large room, filled with people sitting at desks with computer screens, separated from one another by thin, flimsy, white partitions. I dodged around the partitions, the mini-recording device tightly clutched in my sweaty right hand.

'Stop her!' yelled the security guard, reaching the entrance to the floor.

A tall skinny guy with glasses made a grab for me but I ducked under his outstretched arms and continued running, unsure what direction to try. I caught sight of a glass door and swung right towards it. A few seconds later, I reached the door and pushed, then pulled, but it wouldn't budge.

'Stop running!' called the security guard from close behind me.

I spun around and ran off in the opposite direction. Half-way down an aisle, I tripped on a potted plant and grabbed at the corner of a desk to stop myself falling, sending stacks of papers and pens and boxes of paperclips crashing to the floor.

'Hey!' yelled a red-haired woman sitting at the desk.

'Sorry! I gasped, starting to run again.

The security guard was so close now he could almost touch me. I reached another door and again it was locked. I pushed a red button at the side and the door slid open and I bounded inside. I found myself in a large room with white-painted walls, filled with nothing but large plastic rubbish bins. There was no way out except the way I came in, which was now blocked by the bulky security guard.

'Calm down, kid,' he said advancing towards me. 'There's nowhere left to run.'

I looked frantically around me. Without pausing to think, I opened the steel grey trap door and hurled myself into the rubbish chute, feet-first. I felt a hand grab me by the collar of my cardigan and, after a brief struggle, I pulled free and began to hurtle downwards at a pace way faster than any ride at *Great Adventure*.

Chapter 28

'Owwwwwwwww!' I exclaimed, as I landed with a heavy bump in a large metal rubbish skip filled with black plastic garbage bags. I scrambled to my feet, slipping on the plastic and rubbing my very sore head. I wondered if I had a bald patch where I'd cut my hair when I got trapped in the chute. My legs were shaking but I didn't appear to have broken anything. I hauled myself to the top of the skip and peeped over the top. Nobody was in sight. I appeared to be in the basement of the building. I dragged myself up and over the top of the skip, losing the two middle buttons from my cardigan in the process. Letting myself hang down and preparing to drop to the ground on the other side, I thought gratefully of last summer's tree-climbing practice.

This morning felt like a million light years ago.

I made my way across the basement and opened the heavy steel door cautiously and peered around it. Brilliant. It led directly outside, around the corner from the main entrance to Leela's office building. I walked out into a day that had turned almost as dark as night and quickly made my way around to the front of the building, where I spotted Kylie and Ben on the corner, hiding behind a plastic and glass bus-stop shelter. Kylie waved frantically at me just as a very large and very bald security guard grabbed hold of me. He spun me around to face Leela.

'That's the one!' said Leela to him. 'She's the daughter of a client of mine and she stole a tape from my office. Her poor mom doesn't know what to do with her, she's been in and out of trouble with the police for stealing since she was seven years old.'

'That's all total lies, I swear!' I said to the security guard, but he didn't appear to be listening as he was too focused on admiring the sexy lace black camisole that Leela was wearing under her now unbuttoned suit jacket.

'She's holding the tape in her hand,' Leela said to him in a voice that sounded a lot more like a little girl's than mine did.

The security guard prised open my clenched right fist, retrieved the mini-recorder with the tape still inside and handed it over to Leela.

'Thank you, officer,' she said, sweetly.

Out of the corner of my eye, I spotted Kylie holding up her hand to her ear in a phone sign. I knew what she was asking. Should she call Scott? I shook my head slightly. She pointed at herself and then at Leela and waited. I nodded my head slightly. Yes, she understood. I stuck out the three middle fingers on my right hand and mouthed the count-down. Kylie watched me intently and on three, she sprang into action with a speed that made the purple streak in her hair blur.

'Owwwwww…' yelled Leela, as a ninety pound girl-whirl

197

pushed her with all her might so that Leela landed on her well-rounded backside on the pavement. At the same time, I pulled as hard as I could to free myself from the security guard as Ben launched himself at his ankle.

'What the hell?' said the security guard, as Ben's teeth sank into a painfully fleshy part of his leg, causing the guard to release his grip on me.

'Run, Evie!' yelled Kylie, and, grabbing Leela's bag from the pavement, I pulled out the recorder, tossed the bag back and legged it up the block, catching up with Kylie at the corner.

'Ben,' I gasped, looking back. The security guard had got hold of him by his collar and was shaking him like a rat. Ben yelped in pain and frustration.

'We have to go back for him,' I said, already running back.

'Ben!' I yelled. 'Ben, come here, boy. You can do it.'

With a superdog effort, Ben slipped his head through his collar and ran up to me and began licking my outstretched hand. The security guard started to run towards us, calling to another guard to 'go for the little Chinese girl'.

Kylie pulled me by my cardigan. I might as well bin that rag by this stage, I thought. The three of us headed uptown, zigzagging through the crowds, Ben acting like we were in the middle of a glorious game of chasing a cyberball.

'TAXI!' screamed Kylie, pointing at a yellow cab just ahead, its door open as a lady in a red bikini top with shorts stepped out. She smiled and held the door open for us. Kylie dived in first, with Ben and me on her heels.

'77th and Central Park West, as quick as you can!' I gasped.

'We're being chased,' said Kylie, 'by a racist pig security guard.'

The cabbie turned his turbaned head in our direction.

'No problem,' he said, and looking at me, he added, 'are you ok, kid?'

'Fine,' I said, 'more than fine.'

Chapter 29

As the cab made its way uptown, the long-threatened storm finally broke with a magnificent rumble of thunder and a series of dramatically streaked flashes of lightning. There were a couple of moments of eerie stillness when even the yellow taxis stopped honking their horns and then, a whooshing, crashing sound as the rain pounded down.

I pressed my face up against the misty window of the cab. This was completely different to the soft, lazy drizzle of Irish rain. This rain was so heavy that it sounded like it had murder on its mind. We stopped on the east side to drop Kylie off at her mom's gallery.

Finally, the cab reached home. I dashed down the steps, tore past Karen sitting behind the reception desk, dripped my way down the corridor and reached the examining room, startling Joanna and Angel, the small yellow canary in her hands, which chirped and beat its little wings rapidly.

'Where's Scott?' I panted.

'Are you training for the marathon, Evie? Scott's on his way to lunch with Leela.'

'A special lunch,' she added.

'What?' I said, horrified.

'Evie, breathe! I didn't mean to scare you. You should change out of that soaking dress. Apparently, Scott told Jake last night that he was going to break up with Leela today. Jake told Sidney, who told me, and she specifically asked me to tell you; she said it was important that you know.'

'What?' I said again, leaning back against the wall.

'You heard me,' said Joanna, puzzled. 'Leela and Scott are no more, or at least, they will be no more by this afternoon.'

I stared at her with my mouth open.

'Don't look at me like that,' said Joanna. 'I'm trying hard not to be too celebratory.'

'No, no, it's not that,' I said. 'It's … I have to go.'

'What happened to your hair?' asked Joanna. 'There's a big clump missing.'

'Oh, em, it's a long story. I have to go. See you later,' I said, backing out the door.

I towel-dried Ben and gave him three slices of salami from the refrigerator. Then I lifted him up, carried him into my room and began to wait for Scott. It felt like the afternoon lasted an entire weekend, the tedium broken only by texting with Kylie and Greg and by keeping Ben's mind off the storm raging outside my window. I felt nervous about what kind of lies Leela might be telling Scott but I reminded myself over and over that I had the mini-recorder with tape intact.

At last, at around six, Ben perked up his ears, jumped off my bed and headed out the door. I quickly followed. Scott opened the front door to the apartment, set down a damp brown paper bag of food on the kitchen counter and stooped to greet Ben, scratching him behind the ears.

'Hi,' I said, nervously.

'Hi,' he said, as if nothing unusual had happened. 'I've got empanadas for dinner, spicy chicken, cheese and chorizo. Take your pick.'

Together we laid out plates and forks and knives and glasses of iced water. It was maddening the way Scott kept yakking on about inconsequential things; he was finally going to fix his Harley motorbike, and he needed to order some more heartworm pills for dogs as stock was running low, and would the rains flood the entrance to the basement clinic?

'How was your day?' he asked, as we finished eating.

'Um, ok,' I said, watching him for a reaction.

He put down his napkin and said, 'I have something to tell you.'

'Yes,' I said, trying not to sound too eager.

'Leela and I broke up today. It was time.'

'Oh,' I said, 'are you ok?'

He broke into a lopsided grin.

'I'm fine,' he said. 'I think Leela and I … I think our relationship had run its course. She'll be much happier with someone who is …'

'Richer?' I suggested.

'I was going to say more like she is, but richer would help.'

'Did Leela mention me or anything about this morning?' I asked.

'No,' said Scott. 'What about this morning?'

Now was the time to present the tape from the mini-recorder to Scott, but I hesitated. I didn't need it anymore.

I should give it to him anyway, I thought. I mean, I did go to quite a lot of trouble to get it.

Know when to use your words, I thought.

Know when words are not necessary, another voice echoed in my mind.

'Mum,' I said.

'What?' said Scott.

I smiled at him.

'I was just thinking about Mum,' I said. 'I think Janet was right. I think Mum watches over me sometimes.'

'And is she happy about you going back to Ireland?' he asked.

'No!' I said, immediately, and I knew that was true.

'So, your mum would want you to stay, and Leela is out of our lives for good. How about you reconsider and decide to stay?' asked Scott.

I stared down at my plate with one, lonely, half-eaten empanada left, and I had a horrible, panicky thought.

'Scott, you didn't break up with Leela because of me, did you?'

Scott laughed.

'No. I mean, I don't think you and Leela were destined to be BFFs as Kylie would say, but that was only a small part of it. I have gone out with so many Leelas, I lose track. I thought maybe it was time for change. So, what

203

do you say about staying?'

He waited, but I said nothing.

He sighed, got up and began clearing away the mess. As I got up to help, I felt a big, empty, hollow cave in my stomach like I hadn't eaten in weeks.

Chapter 30

The next morning, my third last morning in America, I found Scott with Finn and his parrot, Kurt, in the examining room.

'I don't know what's up with Kurt. He's not himself,' said Finn.

'Birds often try to hide their illnesses, because in the wild a sick bird can get pushed out of the flock,' said Scott. 'Try to think about what you mean when you say he is not himself.'

'Well,' said Finn, thoughtfully, 'he's lethargic and he seems a little off balance. He has stopped being rude to people. It's probably nothing but a big waste of your time.'

'No,' said Scott. 'It's never a waste of my time. You did the right thing bringing him in. Let's take a look. Can you take him out of his cage for me?'

The phone in the reception room rang and rang without Karen answering it.

'Evie, can you get it?' asked Scott.

I galloped up the corridor to the reception area and picked up the phone. The caller wanted to make an appointment to get her cat spayed. I took down all the details impatiently, and scheduled the appointment. As soon as I hung up, the phone rang again. It was a man with a hoarse voice, asking if we sold exotic fish.

'Sorry, this is a veterinary practice,' I told him. 'Try a pet store,' and I hung up.

When I finally made it back to the examining room, Finn's face was blank and his mouth was set in a hard, straight line. He thanked Scott and he left with Kurt, only barely saying goodbye to me.

Scott began to scrub down the table.

'What is it?' I asked. 'What's wrong with Kurt?'

Scott put the rag down.

'Pacheco's disease. It's a virus.'

'But he's going to be okay, right?' I asked.

'I don't know,' he answered. 'Pacheco's disease is usually fatal, but there has been some success with a drug called acyclovir, so we are treating him with that. We'll have to wait and see.'

'Oh,' I said, 'but where there's life, there's hope, you know, like Joanna says.'

'There's always hope, Evie, but I'm not going to lie to you. It's not likely that Kurt will survive. If he makes it through the night, I asked Finn to bring him back in the morning.'

'Isn't there anything more we can do? I asked. 'Can I do something? Anything?'

Scott shook his head.

'I wish there was, Evie.'

The rest of the day dragged. I ping-ponged between Scott and Joanna, pestering them with more and more questions and arguments like, 'if Kurt is still alive *now*, does that mean he's going to make it?' and half an hour later, 'if Kurt is still alive *now*, does that mean he's going to make it?'

Finally, Scott got exasperated.

'Evie, I don't know, I can't know. We have to wait.'

'I think he's going to make it,' I announced.

'Kurt is a very, very sick parrot,' Scott replied.

Although Finn never talked much about Kurt, I knew he loved him. I remembered my first night in New York, how alone and unloved I felt and how Ben's warm presence comforted me. It didn't seem important anymore that Finn didn't like girls like me who think too much. I shifted from pestering Scott and Joanna to bugging Greg.

'Please text me an update every half an hour,' I begged.

I went to bed early to try to make the next morning come around faster, but I couldn't sleep.

At about nine-thirty, Scott knocked softly on my door.

'Evie, are you awake?'

'Yes,' I called out, sitting up in bed and switching on the bedside lamp. As soon as I saw Scott's face, I felt like putting my pillow over my head, because I didn't want to hear what he had to say.

'Finn called. Kurt died about half an hour ago.'

'I can't believe it,' I said.

But I could believe it. I punched my pillow.

'I think Kurt is the only pet that Finn ever had. It's not fair.'

Scott sat down beside me on the bed, and for a few

moments, we stayed in silence, each of us thinking our own thoughts.

'Finn's sure that Kurt is dead, right? I mean, he's not just in a deep sleep.'

'Kurt's gone, Evie,' said Scott.

I hunched my knees up and wrapped my arms around them and rocked slightly back and forth, an old habit from when I was little.

'Mum's dead,' I said loudly.

'Yes,' said Scott.

'She's not coming back, you know,' I whispered.

'No, she's not,' he said, quietly.

'It's so not fair,' I said.

'It's not fair,' he agreed.

'Evie, it's not your fault.'

I felt a wave, a giant tidal wave, a tsunami of grief welling up deep inside me and I hid my face on Scott's new baby-blue cotton shirt. Soon I noticed it felt damp and no longer crisp, but sodden and wrinkled, but Scott didn't mind. He hugged me until my tears stopped running, which was a very long time.

And when I had finished and blew my nose and hiccupped a little and wiped my face with some tissues, he said, 'Get some sleep,' and I slept.

Chapter 31

The next morning was my second last day. Kylie came over to help me pack. I told her she didn't have to, but she insisted.

'I love a project,' she told me.

She arrived with highlighters, stickers, and squares of soft, tissue packing paper, which she laid out carefully on my bed. I thought of my pair of grubby runners.

'I'm not sure I need all this,' I said.

'Yes, you do,' she said. 'There's an art to packing.'

'I usually just open my suitcase, throw everything in, squeeze stuff in at the top and then sit on it to close it,' I pointed out.

Kylie looked horrified.

'It's a crime to treat clothes like that, even clothes like yours. Now, pass me all your shoes first; they should go at the bottom.'

I complied listlessly.

'This is the pile of the clothes that, trust me, you don't want to keep. You can donate them to charity,' she said, pointing at a heap on the bed at the top of which she had added my very scruffy denim shorts.

I began to sort through the pile, taking items out.

'Will all of your friends be in school with you?' she asked, putting my denim shorts very firmly back into the donation pile.

'No, we'll be starting secondary school now, which is like your high school, except we start when we are twelve or thirteen. Most of my old friends are going to an all-Irish school on the north side of Dublin, but Janet has moved in with Brendan in Bray, which is too far away, so I will go to the local secondary school there and I won't know anyone.'

'Not knowing anyone stinks. If you stayed here, you could go to school with Greg and me!' exclaimed Kylie.

'I'm used to starting new schools,' I assured her.

'Are you taking Sam on the plane with you?' she asked.

I glanced over at Sam, happily sunning himself on the window ledge.

'No,' I said. 'Scott doesn't think that would be fair to him. We're going to put him back in Turtle Pond in the Park in the morning.'

'That's so sad,' she said. 'Are you sure you have to leave?'

I nodded.

'I can't bear being a money-sucking leech, driving the clinic out of business.'

'You should talk to Scott about it,' she urged. 'You're such a big fan of using words. Why don't you use your words now?'

'Sometimes, there are no words,' I said, feeling very grown up.

She looked doubtful.

'Can I have the tape of Leela? Greg wants to hear it.'

'Sure,' I said.

'We're both coming with you and Scott to the airport tomorrow.'

'Thanks,' I said, giving her a big hug.

I ate lunch with Joanna on a bench in the Park, near the lake. We had sandwiches; a turkey club, easy on the mayo for me and a chicken salad wrap for her. We watched tourists clumsily rowing little boats on the lake. An old man and an old woman kissed and the man dropped one of the oars into the lake and the woman laughed.

'I have an older sister and two older brothers. I always wanted a little sister,' Joanna said. 'And you are like a little sister to me.'

I felt tears pricking at the back of my eyelids and I sniffed and dashed them back.

'For a long time, I couldn't cry at all. Now I cry all the time,' I said.

'It gets worse when you get older,' Joanna replied, 'and it happens at the oddest times. Back in April, a cat died on the operating table, during a routine operation. I was devastated, but not as devastated as the owner. Poor Mrs Allingham, that cat was all she had. But I didn't cry. I had to be professional. And later that night, the man behind me in the line at the drugstore snapped at me and said, "Hurry up, lady," when I was struggling to find my purse in my bag and I just started crying. I dumped my stuff on the counter and I left.'

I nodded sympathetically.

'You have to follow your heart, Evie,' she said. 'Is your heart telling you to go to Ireland?'

I thought about that. I didn't want to hurt Scott by having him waste all his money on me, so I think that was coming from my heart.

'Yes, I think so,' I said.

'We will miss you.'

'And I'll miss you, all of you. You have to take care of Scott. He falls asleep on the sofa watching TV and wakes up with a stiff neck if someone doesn't wake him up and make him go to bed. And he never remembers to buy toilet paper so we are always running out and we have to use the cotton pads from the clinic, the ones for cleaning out the big dogs' ears, so if you remind him about the toilet paper, that would help.'

'Scott, get toilet paper? I can do that,' said Joanna.

We strolled back through the Park, around the Great Lawn and past Turtle Pond and out the West 77th Street entrance. As we waited to cross the street, we watched all the kids coming out of the Natural History Museum with their friends and their parents and they looked happy.

Joanna headed straight in to the clinic and I went up to the apartment.

'Tomorrow's the big day,' said Frank in the lobby.

'Yep,' I said.

'We're going to miss you, Beautiful, and your real nice manners.'

'I'll miss you too,' I said. I finished packing.

Ben sat on the floor with his head in his paws and watched me intently, following my every move. I couldn't quite look him directly in the eyes.

At last, when everything was zipped up, I wandered out to the kitchen. Scott was sitting on one of the bar stools, tapping something small in his right fist against the glass table – clink, clink, clink.

'Sit down, Evie,' he said, patting the bar stool beside him.

I sat.

'It's the money. You're worried about money. Leela convinced you that you are bankrupting me and the clinic.'

I looked up at him.

'Well, em…' I stuttered.

'Evie,' he said, looking excited, 'you are being so dumb. The money is a non-issue. We'll make it work. The clinic is getting busier all the time. Joanna and I want to expand it so we will have a bigger surgery and room for more surgical equipment. Then, we can carry out more operations. And I'm going to make Joanna a partner.'

He continued in a rush, 'Evie, you are the only family that Ben and I have. What would we do without you? Who will remember about buying toilet paper?'

'Are you sure about the money?' I said. 'It seems to be a lot cheaper to be a kid in Ireland.'

Scott laughed and grabbed my hands and pulled me up from my stool and swung me around.

'Sure I'm sure,' he said. 'You'll stay, won't you?'

I nodded.

'Come on, let's go downstairs and tell Joanna the good news.'

'How did you find out?' I said.

He waved the tape around and put it in his pocket.

'Finn gave this to me today.'

'Finn! Finn Winters!' I said.

'Yes.'

'I can't believe it! I can't believe Greg gave the tape to him. We had an agreement, me, Kylie, Greg, everything stayed with us and just us.'

'Don't blame Greg,' said Scott. 'Finn told me he overheard Greg playing it and he stole it.'

'He's a smart kid,' added Scott, and then, as an afterthought, he said, 'Not that stealing is right!'

I didn't know what to think, or to say.

'I'm going over to see Leela tonight and she's not going to be torturing any kids anymore. In fact, she will probably find herself out of a job,' Scott added in his most serious voice, with the angriest look I have ever seen in his eyes.

I almost felt sorry for Leela.

I walked across the floor.

'It's such a huge thing that I'm staying, right, Scott?'

'Huger than huge,' he said.

'So, it's almost practically like an emergency situation,' I said, looking longingly at the fireman's pole.

He laughed.

'Just this once, come over here, we'll slide down together.'

I leaned forward in front of Scott and put both hands tightly on the pole. He put his arms around me and the pole.

'Ready?'

I nodded.

WHOOOOSSSSSSSH. It was brilliant fun although we scared the hell out of a nervous looking cat when we crash-landed at the bottom.

The noise drew Joanna out of the examining room and she observed Scott and me sprawled on the floor.

'Hi, kids,' she said, drily.

'It's an emergency,' said Scott. 'Evie, tell her the news!'

After we celebrated with Joanna, and I had called Kylie and Greg, we called Janet about me staying on in America and, once reassured that this is what I wanted, she was tearful, but happy for me. She said that she and Brendan would come to New York on a holiday at Christmas and that I could go visit them next year and go down to Dingle with them for the summer.

I called Deirdre and Cate as well and we agreed that we would always remain friends, no matter what.

Chapter 32

Most of the rest of the week was taken up with doing interviews and placement tests for four different schools. It was nerve-racking and I hoped I got into the same school as Greg and Kylie. This morning, Scott got a letter from one of the schools offering me a place in the seventh grade, but still no word from St Sebastian's.

'You're going to need tutoring to bring you up to speed on American history,' Scott said, reading the letter from the first school.

'Ok,' I said.

'And apparently you are way behind on social studies. How did that happen?' he asked.

'What are social studies?' I asked.

'And there is the answer,' he said.

Kylie came over and we took Ben for a walk in Riverside Park for a change. We bumped into Tamara walking Patrick.

'He's gotten *so* big!' I said.

She smiled.

'He's still not toilet trained. Last night, he did a big dump in one of my dad's shoes and he had a fit.'

'Evie sat the placement test for Sebs,' announced Kylie.

'Good luck!' said Tamara. 'Camille goes there too. She's my cousin, but she can be such a brat sometimes.'

'Yeah,' said Kylie. 'She told us that Finn said he doesn't like Evie because she thinks too much.'

'*Kylie*,' I thundered, 'that's private; it's nothing, Tamara.'

'What are you guys talking about?' Tamara said in a puzzled voice. 'That's not what Finn said. I remember it clearly because he got so mad; you guys know how he can lose it. We were hanging out at Aunt Joan's pool in the Hamptons. Camille said something mean about Evie looking like a scrawny scarecrow… Oops, sorry, Evie, and Finn lashed out at her and said, "she's a thinker". Then Akono, who was Julius Caesar in his drama club last winter, said, "She has a lean and hungry look, she thinks too much, such women are dangerous …" or something like that. I'm not sure, but it was a quote, or he was paraphrasing, or something, and that was it. I guess Camille put her own, unique, dark twist on it.'

'Oh,' I said.

Tamara smiled at me and said, 'I'm sure Finn likes you, Evie. He thinks you are a sweet kid.'

'And funny,' she added.

I thought I would prefer if Finn didn't like me at all rather than think I was a sweet, funny kid, but I just said, 'thanks.'

'Camille wasn't always this bad' said Tamara. 'You guys know that Uncle Andre spent the whole summer in France and he's divorcing Aunt Joan.'

'No, we didn't know,' said Kylie.

I felt a ripple of sympathy for Camille.

'I have to go,' said Tamara. 'Good luck with getting into Sebs, Evie. Call me if you need any help.'

The atmosphere in the clinic that afternoon was light and giddy and special, just like the last day of school before summer. Joanna and Scott were treating an anxious- looking roan and black Great Dane called Dodger. They teased one another and laughed a lot. I thought that we didn't need the lights on because Joanna was so radiant that she could have powered the entire building.

Joanna held Dodger down while Scott swabbed his ears to test for infection. Karen walked in as I carefully carried the microscope from the side cabinet towards the table under the window.

'There's a man out there who wants to see Evie,' she announced in a peculiar voice.

'Who is he?' Scott asked casually, pulling the swab of cotton wool out of Dodger's left ear.

Karen hesitated.

'Who is he?' Scott repeated, looking up.

Karen looked confused.

'He says he's her father,' she said slowly.

A heartbeat later, there was a massive commotion as Scott and Joanna both jumped forward at the same time to catch me before I hit the floor, managing to whack their heads together. The microscope crashed to the ground, sending a thousand shards of glass and metal flying through the air, and Dodger grabbed the opportunity to leap from the table in a single bound, knock down a shelf containing fifty-five cans of dog food and dash out the exit.

But I only found out about all that later. I have never fainted before. I wouldn't recommend it, but I can say it was a very interesting experience.

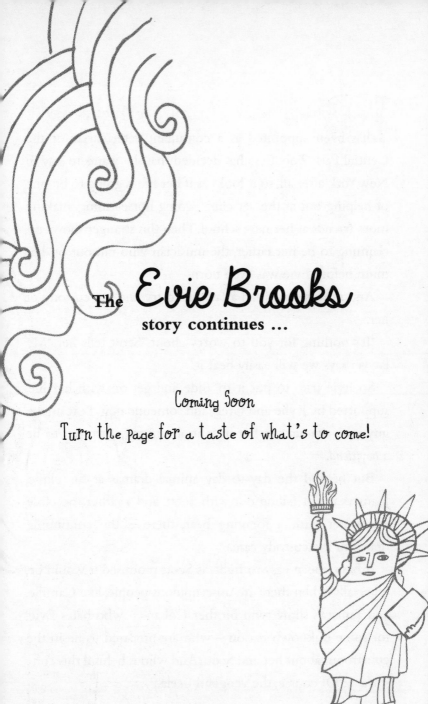

The *Evie Brooks*
story continues ...

Coming Soon
Turn the page for a taste of what's to come!

Everything was almost perfect. Scott has been appointed as a consultant veterinarian at the Central Park Zoo. Evie has decided that she wants to stay in New York after all, so it looks as if her life is going to be one of helping out at the vet clinic, going horse-riding, making more friends at her new school. Then this stranger shows up, claiming to be her father, the musician who ran out on her mum before Evie was even born.

And now he has filed a lawsuit to try and get custody of her.

'It's nothing for you to worry about,' Scott tells her. 'My lawyer says we will easily beat it.'

So Evie tries to put it to aside and get on with her life, supported by Kylie and Greg, and someone new, Lorcan, the guy who sits next to her in school, and may turn out to be a *boyfriend*.

But behind the day-to-day animal dramas at the clinic, Joanna's major falling out with Scott, and a rather too close encounter with a foraging bear, there is the continuing drama of the custody case.

It hasn't been easy to fight, as Scott promised it would be, especially when there are unscrupulous people, like Camille, and Tamara's slimy twin brother Coltan – who hates Evie, for some unknown reason – who are prepared to lie in the courtroom about her and Scott. And who is behind this conspiracy? Of course, the vengeful Leela.

How will it all turn out? Will Evie really have to go to live in Australia with her father?